# PABLO CARTAYA

PUFFIN BOOKS

# WANT TO READ MORE BOOKS BY PABLO CARTAYA?

Don't Miss These Titles

PUFFIN BOOKS
An imprint of Penguin Random House LLC, New York

First published in the United States of America by Kokila,
an imprint of Penguin Random House LLC, 2019
Published by Puffin Books, an imprint of Penguin Random House LLC, 2020

Visit us online at penguinrandomhouse.com

THE LIBRARY OF CONGRESS HAS CATALOGED THE KOKILA EDITION AS FOLLOWS:
Names: Cartaya, Pablo, author.
Title: Each tiny spark / by Pablo Cartaya.
Description: New York: Kokila, [2019] | Summary: Sixth-grader Emilia Torres struggles with
ADHD, her controlling abuela, her mother's work commitments, her father's distance after
returning from deployment, evolving friendships, and a conflict over school redistricting.
Identifiers: LCCN 2019013145 | ISBN 9780451479723 (hardback)
Subjects: | CYAC: Fathers and daughters—Fiction. | Attention-deficit hyperactivity disorder—
Fiction. | Family life—Georgia—Fiction. | Middle schools—Fiction. | Schools—Fiction. |
Hispanic Americans—Fiction. | Georgia—Fiction. | BISAC: JUVENILE FICTION /
People & Places / United States / Hispanic & Latino. | JUVENILE FICTION / Family / Parents. |
JUVENILE FICTION / Social Issues / Prejudice & Racism.
Classification: LCC PZ7.C24253 Eac 2019 | DDC [Fic]—dc23
LC record available at https://lccn.loc.gov/2019013145

Puffin Books ISBN 9780451479747

Printed in the United States of America

7 9 10 8 6

Design by Jasmin Rubero
Text set in Fiesole Text

To Penelope, Leonardo, and Paloma,
who teach me something new and remarkable
every single day

"When we wake up in the morning, we can choose between fear and love. Every morning. And every morning, if you choose one, that doesn't define you until the end. . . ."

—Guillermo del Toro

# EMILIA'S VIDEO
## #30

The camera light blinks like a winking red eye, telling me it's time to start. I take a short breath. I know each detail of my face is being recorded—every eyebrow movement, every twitch. What if the spinach smoothie I just drank left little green flecks in my teeth? My stomach swirls like the red, white, and blue sign outside of Butch's Barbershop. The one off Main Street. Right next to Delucci's, my favorite restaurant.

"Emilia?"

"Hmm?"

"We're recording," Gus says in a whisper.

What am I going to say? Even though I've done this twenty-nine times, I feel like I should have written a script. I stare straight into the lens. Gus watches quietly behind the camera. Focus, Emilia. Breathe.

And:

Hi, Papi! It's me, Sweet E. Emilia Rosa. Your daughter. You know that. So, how are you doing? I miss you. I had a good birthday. Abuela made flan de coco. You like flan, right? Abuela signed me up for piano lessons, but I'm not very good. She says I just have to practice. I'd rather join the makers club at school. They're going to teach kids how to wire-circuit boards. Mom says it's a great idea. But part of me wonders if I'd get bored because I'm already good at circuit boards. Remember? Mom showed me. It was pretty easy. So, I, well, is it cold where you are? Is it in the mountains this time? I miss you, Papi. Oh, hey! I drew something for you. Here, see? It's like the tattoo you have on your shoulder, only I ran out of green marker. That's why the wings are pink. And that's purple fire coming out of its mouth. Mom said I had creative license to draw the fire whatever color I wanted. Maybe you can use this drawing to get another dragon tattoo? Like on your other shoulder. Right above your Semper Fi one. Anyway, it's for you. I'm going to scan it to send with the video file. I know it's hard for you to Skype where you are, so I hope you get this soon. And the drawing. Bye, Papi. I love you.

**END VIDEO**

# CHAPTER ONE

I wasn't fast enough. Abuela appears behind me, already dressed with her makeup on, hair in a perfect bun. "Ven," she says, holding two brushes and a flatiron. She gestures for me to follow her into her room. I really wanted to get a few knots out of my hair before she got started.

She sits me down on the footstool facing her full-length mirror. As soon as my butt touches the seat, she hammers away with the hairbrush like she's some kind of black-smith hairstylist.

My head jerks as Abuela pulls. She takes a skinny comb with a long, pointy handle and splits my hair into sections with hair clips that look like chomping alligators. With one section in her hand, she takes the flatiron in the other. She feeds my hair into the iron and clamps down on the strands. Steam curls out like a dragon exhaling as the iron slides from the top of my head to my tips. Even though she's never burned me, I get nervous when Abuela gets close to my ears.

I don't have my mom's jet-black hair, but I have her curls. Or waves—my hair swooshes like a rolling tide. But after Abuela's done with it, it's as flat as a pancake. Today she straightens my hair out and puts it up into a ponytail.

"Pa'que se quede liso," she says. I guess she's worried that if I don't put my hair up, it will get wavy later. Abuela turns my head toward the window and keeps working.

There's something comforting about the way the sun enters the room through the curtains in the morning—it's like a *tap-tap-tapping* on the window, telling me it's time to get the day started. A cardinal chirps on the branch of our cedar tree. It flits around, and I'm jealous of the little bird for having so much energy in the morning. I lean over to draw the curtains open and let in more light.

"Quédate quieta, muchacha," Abuela says. "You're moving around too much."

"Aurelia," Mom says, popping into the room. "Déjala con su pelo risado."

Abuela stops tugging and looks back at Mom.

"She's going to go to school with her hair curly and out of control? She won't be able to focus," Abuela says.

"What?" my mom replies. "That's ridiculous."

"Well, what will people think? I'll tell you: that she doesn't have anybody to take care of her. Is that what you want?"

"That's what this is about," my mom says. "It's always about what other people think."

"It's important to put your best foot forward," Abuela says, continuing to brush out my ponytail.

"And I think her wavy hair is beautiful. It's her best foot, and I won't let you tell her otherwise." Mom winks while she scrunches her own hair.

"It's fine, Mom," I finally say.

It's not *really* fine—Abuela's daily hair rituals hurt, and I think my hair is like a lion's mane. And I love lions. But I'm not interested in Abuela and Mom getting into another argument over my hair.

Abuela finishes by putting a large blue bow on top of my head. I get up and move toward my mom, who is still standing at the door. She's wearing baggy sweatpants and a tank top and has her favorite fluffy argyle socks on. Her long, curly black hair falls along her shoulders like a waterfall in the dead of night.

I look back at my grandmother. She's wearing freshly

pressed pants and a blouse with circles and stars on it, her auburn hair perfectly in place without a loose strand. Her round rosy cheeks and thin lips are stained the color of an Arkansas Black apple, and she's wearing the same gold-and-pearl earrings she's worn since my abuelo died.

Between my mother and grandmother, I'm a blend of both. Short, head of wavy auburn hair, eyes large with dark yellow-green colors.

I don't have Mom's complexion. One that, as she once said, shows she is a "descendant of the Yoruba."

"Emilia viene de sangre española," Abuela replied. "She resembles *my* side of the family."

"She may have some Spanish ancestry," Mom said. "But she also has West African blood coursing through her veins. She needs to know *all* parts of her heritage, not just the European one—"

"Bueno," Abuela interrupted. "Remember, most of our family came from Spain. And some from Ireland. That's why your hair is that color, mi'ja."

"Si, pero you can't deny the orishas guide her spiritual journey as well," Mom said.

"Aye, muchacha," Abuela responded, clearly frustrated. "She's baptized Catholic."

"You baptized her Catholic, Aurelia," Mom said. Then she whispered to me loudly enough for Abuela to hear: "No matter what, nunca dudes lo que está in your mind and spirit, mi amor. That, and sea como sea, our Yoruba heritage teaches us to respect your elders."

Mom kissed my forehead.

I smiled. Abuela frowned.

"Come on," Mom says now. "Let's eat breakfast."

"Espérate." Abuela stops me before I head out.

She slathers her hands with gel and smooths the hair at the top of my forehead so it's flat against my scalp. I stare at myself in her full-length mirror as the plastering continues. My eyes follow Abuela's arm to the short cylindrical can she's digging into. Actually, it's pomade she's using. Not gel. Pomade is greasier and stays in my hair longer. It gives it a slick sheen, but honestly, I hate it because it takes forever to wash out. I don't say anything, though.

We walk downstairs, past the dining room that leads into the kitchen. Mom and I start our daily ritual of making café con leche, with a little slice of Cuban toast and melted butter, plus a large glass of my daily spinach-peanut-butter-banana-and-almond-milk smoothie.

"Doctor's recommendations!" Mom says, pouring the last of the smoothie into my glass.

"Why do I have to drink that horrible green monster *every* morning? It leaves specks of green in my teeth."

"It's not that bad! Here, take your fish oil pill."

"I hate that thing!"

"The doctor *did* say it's a natural way to help you concentrate."

Mom tries to add healthy foods into my diet *all* the time. She says it will help with my lack of focus. I think she's just trying to cut out sugar. Which I *love*.

As the coffee brews, the sweet and bitter smell wafts my way. Whoever figured out that those opposite tastes could blend together so perfectly in a coffee drink was a genius.

Mom puts her arm around me, and I lean into her shoulder.

"What's up, *Not-Buttercup*?" she jokes.

I perk up and smile.

I recently saw an old movie called *The Princess Bride* with Mom and Abuela. It's about this princess named Buttercup who falls in love with a guy named Westley. At one point in the movie, they're in a forest and these gigantic rats attack them. Westley falls to the ground while wrestling the rat, but Buttercup doesn't do anything. There's a humongous rat chewing on Westley's shoulder, and Buttercup doesn't even pick up a stick to bash it! She just stands there screaming for Westley to save her. It really annoyed me. Mom and Abuela eyed each other and said they never saw the movie that way.

Mom rubs my shoulder and gives it a squeeze.

"Ready for school?"

"No," I say, looking out the kitchen window, slurping up the last of my smoothie. Mom goes to the toaster and pulls out the warm bread and cuts it in half. Steam rises when she adds butter, and it melts instantly. She moves the knife like she's conducting an orchestra across each slice.

My mouth feels dry, but it's not because I'm thirsty.

"Do you have to leave?" I ask her.

"Yes, baby girl. The conference starts tomorrow."

"But it's, like, a thirty-hour time difference, Mom."

"It's San Francisco, mi amor. Not China. And it's only a little more than a week. Who knows? Something exciting could come of it."

"Like what?" I ask, moving over to help her. I grab a paper towel and start wiping the loose crumbs off the counter.

"We'll see! Anyway, Dad is coming home tonight," she tells me. "You'll get some one-on-one time with him for a few days!"

"And apparently he's okay with your mother leaving even though he's been gone for eight months," Abuela says, stern at the kitchen door. It doesn't seem to faze Mom at all. She's used to what she calls Abuela's "puyas"—side comments meant to get under her skin. Abuela throws shade like a chameleon changes colors.

Mom rubs my forearm and squeezes my hand a little. "Bueno, Aurelia, luckily my husband and I have communicated, and fortunately for both of us, we understand that our jobs may require a certain amount of travel on occasion. As I'm sure you've experienced over the years with his deployments."

Abuela huffs and leaves the kitchen. Mom exhales slowly.

"How do you not get flustered by her, Mom?"

"Patience, mi amor," Mom says. "The older you get, the more important patience becomes."

I glance over at my backpack and think about all the classes I have and how Mom is always there to help organize my work and how I can't let Abuela help me because she won't understand and suddenly I feel the vibrating in my head that happens sometimes when I get nervous. It's like a whole bunch of little bees buzzing around and it's hard to concentrate.

"Mom, who's going to help me with my homework when you're gone?"

"Dad will!"

The calendar Mom and I go over every Monday morning to help me organize the week sits in front of me. Friday is circled with two little stars and a question mark next to it.

"Oh, Mom! Clarissa is having a party on Friday. Can I go?"

"It's Monday, Emilia. And that's not really relevant to our discussion, is it?"

"So?"

"Well, we're talking about your dad coming home tonight and since it's Monday, I think planning for your *school* week is the priority, don't you think?"

"Mom, please don't start that priority–organizational thinking thing again. I know it's Monday."

"Okay, but you have a math—"

"I know! Geez." I take a breath and exhale. Patience . . .
Right.

"Don't make that face," she says.

"What face?"

"The one that looks like you ate day-old bacalao."

Mom drops her upper lip and her eyes sag a little.

"I hate salted cod," I tell her.

"Oye, your ancestors are probably rolling in their graves."

I drop my head onto my mom's shoulder again. When
I lift it, she hands me her mug. "Bueno, at least you like
café con leche."

I take a sip, and everything comes into focus. There is
nothing like café con leche. Nothing.

"C'mon, mi amor. Let's hang out a little before the bus
gets here," she says.

Mom pats my back and heads to the dining room, carrying the café con leche. I follow her with the buttery Cuban
toast and sit at the dining table, where we've done homework together hundreds of times. Probably thousands.
Maybe millions. Abuela moves past us to the kitchen.

"Should we get him balloons or a sign or something?"
I ask.

"No, you know he doesn't like a big welcome like that,"

Mom says. "Be there with a hug and tell him you're glad he's home."

"Well, I *am* glad he's home. I just wish you were going to be home too."

"I know, baby. But this is going to be good. Trust me."

"Yeah, yeah," I say, swinging my feet and munching on toast and talking about the week ahead. She likes to go over my agenda for the week, but it's kind of annoying because sometimes that's all she talks about.

"So, you got it?"

"Hmm?"

"Your stuff for the week, sweetheart," she says. "Math test Thursday. You have a vocabulary test Friday. What do you have for social studies?"

"Oh, Clarissa's party! I can go, right?"

"Emilia," Mom says, using my name like a sharp-edged sword to make her point. "I need to be able to go on this trip knowing you're ready for the week."

"Yes, Mom, you've told me, like, a hundred times!"

"And social studies?"

"What about it?"

"What do you have for Mr. Richt's class this week?"

"I don't know, something. Maybe a test."

"Maybe? Do I have to call?"

"No, Mami! Please, can we just talk about something else?"

She lets out a sigh. "Okay, mi amor. What do you want to talk about?"

I ask her about her trip, where she's going to present this cool new translation app she developed.

"Are you going to speak in front of a ton of people?"

"I hope not!" she says. "I hate speaking in front of people."

"But you have to talk about it."

"Oh, I have no problem talking one-on-one," she says. "I just hate talking in front of big crowds. Me da pánico."

"You won't panic, Mom," I tell her. "It's going to be awesome."

"I hope so. It'll be a game changer."

I hear the bus rounding the corner, rumbling like a grumpy yellow rhino that hasn't had coffee yet. Would a rhino drink café con leche? Probably. I wish I had a remote control that could pause the bus for a moment longer.

"It's time to go, mi amor." Mom gets up and hugs me.

"I'm going to miss you," I tell her. Her curls wrap around

my shoulders like a dark rain cloud that blocks out the sun and cools the sky.

"I'll call when I land," she says, kissing my forehead. "And you call me for *anything*. Okay?"

"I will," I say, getting up and heading to the door.

Abuela comes back into the dining room and hands me a waffle wrapped in a napkin. The syrup drips onto the napkin and the paper sticks to the waffle. I try to peel it off, but the syrup has already glued it in place.

"Tienes que desayunar más," Abuela says.

"Ya comí, Abuela," I reply, showing her my mostly eaten toast.

She shakes her head. "Pero that tiny piece of bread and that green milkshake aren't enough," she says. "You have to have a full stomach at school, Emilia Rosa."

Mom steps in and takes the waffle out of my hand.

"Aurelia," Mom says. "We talked about this, remember? Her doctor suggested eliminating sugar to see what effect it has on her inattentiveness."

"And the café con leche you gave her this morning? That has sugar."

"It has almond milk and a tiny bit of agave in it."

Abuela shakes her head, then lets out a humph before taking the waffle from my mom. "Whoever heard of café con leche with *agave*?" she mutters loudly enough for both of us to hear.

Mom steps around her to hug me one more time. "Don't let her get to you," she whispers. Abuela frowns. Mom kisses me on the nose and playfully pats my side. "Love you, baby."

"Love you too, Mom," I say, heading outside. "Have a good trip."

"Thanks, mi amor."

"Bye, Abuela," I say, quickly pecking her on the cheek and grabbing my backpack.

"Have a good day, mi'ja," she responds.

The bus is already in front of our house when I step outside. Its doors swing open, and I turn back to look at Mom one more time.

Abuela calls out and rushes to the bus before I get on. She holds my head, tucks a few loose strands of hair behind my ears, and tightens my bow.

"Perfect," she says.

I think about taking a deep breath, but I just get on the bus.

It feels like my whole life is changing. Like everything that's normal is becoming the opposite. We've been like this for so long—me, Mom, and Abuela. Now that Mom is leaving and Dad is coming home—with Abuela probably in charge—I'm not sure what to expect.

# CHAPTER TWO

The stench of a dozen body sprays hits me as I walk onto the bus. Like every morning, I greet Mrs. Loretta, the driver. Like every morning, she asks, "How's your mama?" then nods and closes the door before I can answer.

The bus hums impatiently while I walk down the aisle to find my seat. Clarissa's sitting in the middle of the bus, waving at me excitedly.

"Hey, over here!"

She's by herself in a row, patting the empty space next to her. Mrs. Loretta asks me to take my seat, so I pick up my step. Clarissa scoots over toward the window so there's room for me and my backpack.

"Hey, Clarissa," I say.

"How was your weekend, Emi Rose?"

"Good," I say.

"Your daddy home yet?"

"He comes home today."

"Oh my capital *G-O-D*! Are you excited? I bet you are."

"Yeah," I say. My shoulders feel heavy all of a sudden.

"Well, what's wrong?"

"Oh, nothing," I tell her. "I'm excited. Really."

To be honest, I'm nervous now that my papi is coming home after being gone for over eight months. We hardly ever spoke the whole time he was away. But I don't want to have a conversation about that.

Clarissa says something about how amazing my dad is, and if I know where he was deployed, and are there any pictures he sent, and the more she goes on, the more the words blend before fading into my own thoughts.

She gets really emotional talking about my dad. She lost hers overseas when we were little, and whenever my dad comes home, she wants to find out everything about his deployment. The truth is, I don't know much more than she does this time.

Since kindergarten, Clarissa and I have been friends. We used to hang out more in elementary school, but now that we're in sixth grade, it seems like she's just interested in talking about stuff *she* likes. Like my dad and the military, being a substitute mellophone player in pep band, working as a general staff assistant on the yearbook, and throwing "hangs" with a bunch of kids I don't really care to hang out with.

We sit together on the bus to school, and we have homeroom and social studies together. Sometimes she convinces me to go to a "hang," but not every time. That would be exhausting.

Mostly I'm with my friend Gustavo. Gus, for short. He moved here from Alabama about two years ago. His dad works in Abuela's auto shop right behind our house. Sometimes Clarissa gets mad that I'm with Gus so much. I guess that's why I go to her parties. I don't want her to feel like I'm not her friend, even though I wish she would still be into stuff that *I* find fun. Like that summer we binge-watched thirty-nine episodes of *Trollhunters*, and afterward we made swords and shields and vowed to save the troll market from the evil Morgana.

"I invited seventh graders!" she says, interrupting my thoughts. "You're coming, right?"

"Where?"

"To my *hang*, silly!"

"Oh yeah, sure. I think my mom said yes."

Going from fifth grade to middle school is tough. I

know a lot of things have changed, but I can't always tell *what* exactly. It's strange.

My backpack rests half on my lap and half on the seat. Clarissa says something about a guest list, but I notice my math book is popping out in between the two zippers. I have a test on Thursday. Mom said I have to get As or Bs on my tests if I want to hang out with friends on the weekends.

Clarissa talks about her party supplies. She really goes all out—lots of gold balloons, and at least three different donkey piñatas for every party.

"Maybe I'll get a llama piñata this time! I'll bet kids'll *love* that, huh?"

She always has lots of soda. Her playlists include a bunch of rappers from Atlanta. Actually, most of the TV shows she likes now are either filmed or set in Atlanta.

"I'm a die-hard ATL girl," she always says.

Clarissa emphasizes the ATL part, which stands for Atlanta. For Halloween this year she and a couple of kids wore their hair in braids and called themselves ATL's North Side Crew. She thought it was clever. But it was more like she was making a joke to amuse herself.

"Hello?" Clarissa says, tapping my shoulder.

"Hmm?"

"What are you going to wear to my *haaaaang*? I got this spring dress with roses all over it, and I just thought it was perfect because my middle name is Rose, ya know?"

My middle name is Rose also. Actually, it's Rosa—same as my mom's middle name. Emilia Rosa.

"If you get a rose dress, then we can be the two roses!"

On the History Channel, I watched a show about a time in England called the War of the Roses. There were two families fighting for the crown and they had a brutal war for centuries.

"So?" Clarissa leans her shoulder into mine. She's a lot taller than I am. Sometimes I wish I were a bit taller. Clarissa nudges me again and I feel like I'm going to fall off the seat and into the aisle. "You're so tiny, Emi Rose," she says. "You just tumble over with the slightest shove."

"Yeah," I say, not sure what else to tell her. "So, why do you want to invite seventh graders?"

"*Because,*" Clarissa says. "It's almost the end of the year, and I think we need to have some of the more mature kids at the hang. Don'tcha think?"

"Yeah," I say. "I guess so."

Honestly, I don't think it's a good idea to invite older

kids to hang with sixth graders, but I'm not very good at arguing, and I don't want to make Clarissa angry.

"Hey." Clarissa bumps my shoulder again to get my attention. "Did you hear the school board news? They're talking about moving some kids from Park View to *our* school next year?"

"Not really. Why?"

"Well, *my* mom thinks it is *not* a good idea to over-crowd *our* school just because another one is at capacity."

"Won't it make both schools less crowded?" I tell her.

"Bless your heart, Emi Rose. No! It'll just make ours more crowded!"

"Oh," I say, wondering what the big deal is. We barely have students at Merryville Middle anyway.

"And the plan is to move kids from elementary all the way to high school! Here! To Merryville!" Clarissa shouts so loud, it almost makes me cover my ears.

I still don't understand the problem, but Clarissa seems really passionate about it and I'm not in any mood to disagree. I'm already missing my mom and the day hasn't even started.

The bus takes us down a few more streets and in the distance, the MERRYVILLE MIDDLE: HOME OF THE

SCREAMING EAGLES sign comes into view. The same three flags flap in the wind every weekday morning: our nation's flag, our state flag, and our school flag. I don't think Merryville has a town flag. At least, I've never seen it.

Merryville is a small city surrounded by woods tucked into Cherokee County right next to Forsyth County and about a forty-two-minute drive to Atlanta. It's a tiny little blip of a town, and folks around here like the quaintness of it. I've heard Clarissa's mom say that Merryville is one of the last towns the world hasn't barreled into. I'm not sure what that means, exactly.

Atlanta is the opposite—a big city with a busy downtown area. It's both the city of trees and the home of serious traffic. Even still, people drive like they're racing cars.

When my mom takes the I-75, she always speeds up to get past any trucks driving next to us. I just close my eyes and hope we don't get crushed.

"Earth to Emi Rose!" Clarissa says, waving her hands in my face.

"Hmm?"

"You're doing it again."

"Doing what?" I ask.

"Staring out into space! You're acting weird."

"Oh, sorry," I tell her.

Kids call me weird and strange all the time—even Clarissa. I'm not weird or strange; I just have what's called Inattentive Type ADHD, which my doctor says means I have a hard time organizing and paying attention. Sometimes my thoughts wander. Especially when I'm nervous and anxious about something. Like my dad coming home. Or Mom leaving on a trip. But I don't like being called dumb!

Andrew Stockton called me that once during math class because I was looking out the window at the garbage bins and noticed a rat had climbed out of one. I stared at the rodent and was worried that it might get into the cafeteria and then the whole school would be shut down because of a health hazard.

By the time I decided to mention it to my math teacher, Ms. Brennen, Andrew had said, just out of earshot, "How is Emilia in this math class? She should be in math *support* with the other dummies!"

I couldn't stop thinking about the rat. What if it went to the cafeteria for a bite of school lunch? I saw on the bulletin that we were having chicken-fried steak, biscuits, and lumpy gravy that day. What if the rat fell into the fryer and nobody noticed?!

"You poor thing," Clarissa says, staring at me. "You sure you're feeling okay, Emi Rose? You seem more distracted than, well, usual."

"I'm okay." But really, I can feel my mind racing more than most days.

"Well, anyway," Clarissa says, "I think we should both wear rose dresses for my hang."

I nod and face the window across the row as the bus drives by the old train tracks. Trains run through Merryville every hour or so. You can hear the whistle echo through the halls at school and through a bunch of points in town. The river runs just alongside the edge of Main Street. It isn't much of a river, though. More like a plodding stream, but it's pretty when it shimmers.

The bus parks at the drop-off and everyone spills outside. I stop at the big rock near the flagpole. There's a really old plaque drilled into the rock, but I know that it was added to the school entrance recently, because when we did our sixth-grade orientation in the fall, I didn't notice it. The plaque says MERRYVILLE CITY SCHOOL DISTRICT, and it names 1904 as the year the city district was established.

"Thank you, Mrs. Loretta!" I shout.

She nods and waits for the last kids to get off before swinging the doors shut and driving the bus over to the lot where the second Merryville school bus is already parked.

I turn around and spot Gus waving me over. He's talking to his friends Chinh and Barry. Clarissa sees her group of friends gathering at the foot of the school entrance steps.

"Do you want to walk to class, Emi Rose?" she asks.

"I'll catch up with you later," I tell her. I want to say hi to Gus.

She eyes me, then Gus, who politely waves at her, too. She shakes her head and makes her way to her friends.

"I just don't know why a nice boy like Chinh hangs out with Barry and Gustavo. Barry has the worst grades in school. You know he's on probation, right?"

I didn't know, but by the sound of her exaggerated tone, it's probably not true. Barry is just quiet. Sometimes I get quiet when I'm thinking about things. I wonder if Barry has trouble focusing, like I do. Does he go to our school counselor, Mrs. Jenkins, for "check-ins" on his work and his classes, too?

Barry waves Gus off after Gus makes a funny face. They look like they're having a good time.

"And you should be careful with Gustavo, Emi Rose, because I think he lies," she says. "He says he's from Alabama, but he doesn't sound like anyone from Alabama. He barely speaks English."

"He was born and raised in Alabama, Clarissa. And he speaks English *and* Spanish perfectly."

"Doesn't sound like it to me," she says, looking up at the morning sun. "Oh shoot, I forgot my sunscreen! Did you bring some?"

"No. I didn't put any on."

"You should wear sunscreen, Emi Rose. Your skin gets redder than mine."

Clarissa's mom and my mom and Abuela used to take us to swim class during the summer. They'd sit poolside while we swam. Mom had to hand us a tube of aloe once because we got sunburned so bad, it looked like we had red-hot irons for arms.

"How was your weekend?" Gus asks me, starting our patented handshake. A double back tap of the hand into a high five then a drop into a handshake and topped off with a fist bump.

"Not bad," I say. We walk into school. "I hung out and saw a couple of movies with this filmmaker buddy of mine."

"¡Qué padre!" he says. "Seems like a super-brilliant guy."

"Eh," I say jokingly. "He's okay."

"Very funny," he says. "Oh, Barry and I are going to the movies on Friday. Wanna come?"

"I think I have something," I tell him, looking at the calendar on my phone. "Clarissa's party!"

"Ah," Gus says, like he took a bite out of a rotten apple. "That . . . sounds fun?"

"I don't know; it might be. Hey, maybe you can come?"

"Yeah, it doesn't sound like I'm invited, Emilia. Anyway, if you change your mind, movies at Park View Cinemas!"

"Okay," I say. "But if I ask Clarissa to invite you, will you consider it?"

"Consider what?" Barry says, popping in from behind.

"Clarissa's *partay.*"

"G, we've got movie night."

"I know, that's what I told Emilia. Plus, I'm not invited."

"Invited to what?" Chinh walks up without looking away from his phone.

"You're going to slam into a wall one of these days," Gus says.

"Huh?"

"There's obsessed-with-your-phone and then there's Chinh-level obsession."

"I'm not obsessed!" Chinh tries to resist looking at his phone, but he can't help himself.

"Told you," Gus says. Barry laughs.

"It's not a problem; I can quit whenever I want!"

"Yeah, right," Barry says, walking into school with Chinh.

"Later, G!"

"Later, B."

"Later, Chinh," Gus says, waving.

"Hastah lego, G-money."

Gus shrugs. "At least he tries."

"Yes, points for effort." We make our way up the steps and toward the building.

"So, what do you think Mr. Richt's final semester project is going to be?"

"Oh yeah!" I say, thinking I should text Mom and tell her I remembered the social studies homework I have this week. I'll do it later. "I have no idea," I tell Gus.

"That's the exciting part," he says. "El misterio." Gus makes a swooshing motion with his hands like he's a magician. "Come on, Señorita Emilia." He holds the doors open for me. "Another Monday at Merryville Middle awaits."

"After you, good sir," I tell him. "I insist."

"I accept your chivalrous gesture."

We switch places and Gus bows.

Once inside, we watch the other kids move in and out of the hallways.

"Those walls," Gus says. "I mean, do they *all* have to be painted like that?"

Merryville Middle is big into school spirit. Each wall is either the color of a lemon or the blue Atlantic tide rolling in and out of Tybee Beach. There are giant banners with our school mascot, the Screaming Eagle, dangling over each archway. Why it's a Screaming Eagle and not just an ordinary eagle is something I still haven't figured out.

The first time I walked into Merryville Middle, it felt like the walls were yelling at me. At Merryville Elementary, we were just the Hawks and there was one picture of a hawk at the end of a soft-gray hallway. Actually, now that I think about it, I guess it makes sense. Screaming colors for a Screaming Eagle.

We get to homeroom and put our backpacks in our lockers. Mr. Richt is at his desk, like always, reading the *AJC* daily news on his laptop while the rest of the students file into class. Gus and I sit next to each other because his last name is Sánchez and mine is Torres.

"How was the goodbye with your mom?" Gus asks.

"I don't think it's hit me yet. It still just feels like when I get home, she'll be there."

"That makes sense," he says. "Anyway, she'll be back soon, right?"

"Right," I say, suddenly feeling a little queasy. It's like talking about my mom leaving has set a chemical reaction in my gut.

"But look at it this way: your dad will be home," Gus says. "So that's cool."

"Yeah." But that doesn't make the chemical reaction stop. It only gets worse when I think about my mom and add how nervous and excited I am about seeing my dad.

I hope the two feelings don't cause an explosion inside me, like the experiment we tried last year in science class. Our teacher took us outside and poured a half inch of lemon juice into an empty plastic Coke bottle. She added water until it was about half full and then took out a small box of baking soda.

"Does anybody know what will happen once I add the baking soda?" she asked.

Gus said we would have "rain de limón con Coca!" I was the only one who laughed. Our teacher looked confused and told the class to stand back and put on our safety goggles. Then she sprinkled the baking soda into the bottle, sealed it, and shook it like she was really angry. She placed it on the ground and we all watched as the bottle rattled before flying up into the air. Everyone cheered until the bottle exploded and sprayed our teacher with lemon juice.

"My hypothesis was correct, I guess," Gus told me. "Lem-it rain!"

I wish Gus and I were in science together this year. After national testing, I got put in different math and science classes, so I have a separate schedule for some subjects. The strange thing is that Gus and I had really similar scores, but he wasn't reassigned.

Anyway, that's what I am feeling. I don't want my emotions to explode everywhere. Mr. Richt turns on the television in the classroom and two eighth graders appear onscreen behind a desk, looking like news anchors.

"Okay, everyone, morning announcements," Mr. Richt says. "Pay attention."

The eighth graders start off by having us stand for

the Pledge of Allegiance and then a moment of silence. Everyone closes their eyes, but I peek to see if anybody else has their eyes open. Gus lowers his head, like he does at church. Then he slowly turns and makes a scary face where his eyes, nostrils, and mouth go wide—like he's possessed or something.

"Hello, Emilia Rosa," he whispers in a throaty voice. "¡Soy yo!"

"Stop being creepy!" I whisper.

Gus relaxes his face and giggles. When he smiles, his eyes go wide again. But not in a creepy way this time. You can see every shade of brown in them.

The student anchors start again after the Pledge is over. They mention basic news about the country, then news about school, then they talk about all the clubs and activities happening this week.

"Man, I wish I could do AV club," Gus says.

"Why don't you?"

"I don't think I'm good enough yet."

"Are you serious? No one knows more about making movies in this whole town than you do."

"Thanks, amiga."

The announcers say something else and Gus points at the television. "Uh-oh."

I already know what Gus is referring to. I think about the flyers up on the bulletin boards and the posters taped to the walls.

"Get ready, Merryville Middle!" the kid announcer practically sings out. "At the end of the day, we'll be Screaming Eagles!"

Oh no. I can already hear the rumbling and music that will come from the gym. It's the one thing I dislike most about school. My doctor calls this one of my "sensitivities." Sudden loud noises really bother me. They send my head spinning and make me want to hide in the custodian's closet.

We have a pep rally at the end of the day.

# CHAPTER THREE

The bell for first period rings and Mr. Richt turns to the board and starts writing without saying a word. He's a big guy—tall with square shoulders and a perfectly groomed beard. Besides being the middle-school social studies teacher, he's also the junior varsity football, basketball, *and* track coach. I think he likes teaching history best.

"Okay," Mr. Richt says, facing the class. "Some of you in here are on the basketball team."

Richie Barre and Jay Renter pump their fists in the air. Richie is really tall for a sixth grader. I think his mom played college basketball or something. He lives just outside of Merryville. Right near Park View. I know this because that's where Gus lives. And Barry, too—they're neighbors. Everybody knows Jay's family because they own Renters' Lumber Supply with several stores all over Northwest Georgia. Jay is supposed to be in seventh grade, but the administration "recommended" that he repeat sixth. I don't think he cares he's a whole year older than most of us. He likes to use his age to remind us that we should listen to what he says. Nobody really does.

"Yeah, yeah!" Jay cheers.

"Congratulations, Mr. Renter," Mr. Richt says. "But I don't care. All of you are expected to turn in your history project *on time*. Understand? If you play a sport and have practice, if you think you're somehow going to make it on Broadway because you're *acting* in the spring musical . . ."

Clarissa's best friend, Lacey Roberts, waves to Jeff Samuels. They're only in sixth grade but were both cast as supporting leads in the spring production of *Oklahoma!*

"I. Don't. Care," Mr. Richt continues. "This project counts for fifty percent of your grade, and no one gets a pass."

There are a few grumbles in the classroom. Gus watches Mr. Richt intently. Mr. Richt makes eye contact with me. I smile. He doesn't smile back.

"Okay, here is your project."

He turns to the board and writes down the project title:

*The Merryville Tourism Guide*

"All right," he says in his deep voice. "I want you to pretend that you're introducing Merryville to a visitor. What would you tell them about this town? What places should they visit? Pick an aspect of Merryville that you would want someone to experience or maybe it's someone you want them to meet or learn about. Your guide can include places, people, or events. You'll come up with a project proposal, which I will approve, then you will present a final project in front of the class in three weeks. Your proposals are due on Friday."

"How long should the report be, Mr. Richt?" Clarissa asks, raising her hand but not waiting to be called on.

"I didn't say *report*, Miss Anderson," he says, adding, "and your guide can take the form of a poster, a flyer—"

"A film?"

"Yes, Mr. Sánchez, a film would be fine."

"Awesome!" Gus gives a thumbs-up to Barry, who is sitting a few seats away, and then he turns to me for a high five.

"How long does it have to be?" Jay blurts out, sounding completely bored.

"Long enough to be substantial."

"So, really long?" Jay says.

"Don't waste people's time—most important, *mine*. Don't turn in filler or something that you get nothing out of, Mr. Renter."

I would write down the assignment in my folder, but Mr. Richt doesn't offer any specific instructions. There is nothing to tell me what to do or how to do it. I don't like these kinds of assignments. And Mom isn't even here to help me.

Everyone seems to be jotting down ideas already, but all I can do is *tap-tap-tap* my pencil on my notebook.

Maybe Gus and I can work on something together? He always has good ideas. It's like Mr. Richt hears my thoughts, because he makes sure the rules of partnering are clear.

"Partnering is discouraged unless there is a compelling reason to do so," Mr. Richt says to the class. When students ask what that means, he is quick to explain.

"You will present your own proposal for the project at the end of the week," he says. "Once I have thoroughly examined your proposals, I will determine if partnering with a classmate makes sense. And suffice it to say, it won't be because you're friends. Understood?"

We all nod in agreement. Clarissa mouths something

at me. Behind her, Lacey tries to get Clarissa's attention. I think Clarissa wants to talk after class. I face forward, in Gus's direction. He's drawing something in his notebook.

"Oh," Mr. Richt says. "Almost forgot. All of your research has to be conducted in the field."

"How can we do that, Mr. Richt?" Jay asks. "It's not football season."

Mr. Richt sighs and shakes his head. He walks over to Jay's desk and puts a hand on it. "Mr. Renter," he says, "field research does not have to do with football. It means that you will all need to find information at the library, in the town visitors' bureau, at the local businesses, interviewing people who live and work here. Places that you want to share with visitors. Understand?"

Jay nods.

"And," Mr. Richt adds, "I'm going to do something extremely revolutionary here: absolutely no Internet use."

There is a collective gasp from the class.

"How are we supposed to learn anything?" Lacey blurts out.

"The Internet has all the information in the world!" Braden McCarthy cries. "The whole universe!"

"No Internet," Mr. Richt repeats. "Field research.

Library. Town hall. Visitors' bureau. People. Ask questions to actual humans. Not just Google."

Kids in class shake their heads. Nobody seems to like Mr. Richt's idea of "field research." I can't say I blame them. It seems a little ridiculous. Everyone uses the Internet! I look up at Gus to complain, but he's still busy scribbling.

"Everybody got it?" Mr. Richt asks. "Present your ideas on Friday. Your projects are due in three weeks, and your final presentation to the class is due at the end of that week. Okay? And I reserve the right to ask you to share your progress with the class at any moment, so don't leave everything to the last minute."

More grumbles.

"Okay," Mr. Richt says, writing on the board. "Let's start our lesson on local government. Who knows about the school board vote coming up?"

We all start writing down what Mr. Richt says. It's difficult for me to focus. I listen hard, trying to block out everything but his voice. I jot down notes without looking at my notepad, so I can concentrate on the words coming out of his mouth. It doesn't matter if I have some spelling mistakes. That's what Mom says. Just write down what you hear.

"Voting on local measures ensures that the voices of those who vote are heard," he begins. "It affects what our laws are and, in this case, where we go to school. Who knows what redistricting is?"

What makes it onto my paper is:

voting in locl > laws & schols >> re districts

Mr. Richt goes on.

"Our school superintendent, that's the big boss of our school system, has proposed to ease overcrowding and reduce portable classrooms by moving one thousand students from the Merryville neighborhood of Park View to schools located in the heart of Merryville next school year, Merryville Middle among them. Students in grades kindergarten through twelfth grade will be affected by the move. The proposal went to the school board in December and will be ready for a final vote in May. Now, does anyone know how the district chooses which students will move?"

No one speaks up. Everyone is still busy taking notes.

"It depends on where these students live," he says. "In the simplest terms, that's what redistricting is. The government has a big city map that they've divided into zones that determine where you go to school. They'll redraw those zones."

Clarissa raises her hand and speaks. "But how do they decide how to redraw the map? Do we get a say?"

"Excellent question, Miss Anderson. There will be a public forum to discuss the redistricting. That's a resident's opportunity to voice their opinion. Overall, I believe this is going to be great for the whole community. . . ." Mr. Richt continues. But honestly, I lose track of what he's saying.

He hands out a flyer with details about the proposal. Some students nod as they read it and others shake their heads. I start thinking of my dad coming home and suddenly I get nervous and wonder where Mom must be at this moment. Maybe she's landed in Phoenix? She had two connections. She complained about that this morning.

Outside the window, gray encircles the sky. I hope there isn't turbulence on Mom's flight. I flew once to visit my dad on base in San Diego and the plane suddenly dropped. It felt like my stomach was loose inside my body. The captain said something about "experiencing some turbulence." I didn't like it.

"Okay, everybody got it?"

I watch Mr. Richt then stare at my notes.

Prk View > studnts > 1000 > ?

What a mess. I can barely make out a thing. I put my head down.

There are twenty-nine students in my class and there are three sixth-grade classes in total, with an average of twenty-seven students in each class. Does Merryville have enough interesting things for approximately eighty-one student tourism guide projects? I wonder if Park View Middle is doing the same project. They have *way* more students than we do!

When class is over, Mr. Richt stops me and asks me if I need some guidance on my project.

"I'm okay," I tell him.

"You sure?" he asks. "Remember, your mom said to ask if you have any questions in class. That's what I'm here for."

"Yeah," I say. "I got it. Thanks, Mr. Richt."

"I'm excited to see what you come up with, Miss Torres."

I have absolutely no idea what to do for my project,

but how on earth can I tell Mr. Richt? He would just send a note to my mom explaining that I need more help, then Mom would worry and get distracted from her presentation, and if she has to speak in front of a lot of people, she's going to mess up because she's worried about me and my social studies project. I can figure it out. Maybe.

"Miss Torres?"

"Uh-huh," I say, and smile, hoping he'll let me leave soon.

"Have a good rest of your day."

School has just started, and already I feel overwhelmed.

Two cheerleaders in uniform skip past me, and I remember that there's going to be a pep rally today. I have the rest of the week to think about the social studies project. But right now I have to see how I'm going to get out of the pep rally during last period.

# CHAPTER FOUR

I have zero luck getting out of the pep rally. My science teacher, Mrs. Peters, *loves* them. She takes the class to the gym. I hesitate a few moments but am swept up as everyone pours out into the halls.

"Come on, y'all. Time to get your pep on!" she cries out.

I like Mrs. Peters when she's teaching. But I really don't like when she leads us down the halls to the terror of pep that awaits inside the gym, trying to pump us up along the way.

My brain starts doing somersaults as we get closer.

*Stomp. Stomp. Stomp.*

Every time the gym door opens, I can hear feet in the stands and it reminds me of all the festivals and parades that happen all year long here in Merryville. The biggest and loudest being the annual Fourth of July parade.

Fireworks make me panic. Clarissa says singing "Happy Birthday" to America shouldn't bother me, but it does. My doctor says I process some sensory details differently than other people, so when there is a ton of noise around, it's like my mind becomes a clown car filled with clowns. I don't like clowns very much. They scare me. The Fourth of July celebration in Merryville is like one giant clown car barreling down Main Street. It's hard to keep my brain from running away with the circus.

I don't want to add the Fourth of July Festival to my Merryville tourism guide. What if someone visits and doesn't like loud noises, like me?

I spot Gus walking down the hall, but I stay a few paces behind because I still might run away. There's a song playing, but it's tough to hear what it is with all the students screaming.

"Who has a pep rally on a *Monday*?" I ask Gus, catching up to him.

"What?!" Gus responds.

I put my hands over my ears. "Please don't yell like that," I tell him.

"Sorry!" He can't help it. "Hey, you sure you want to go inside?"

"You know how much I love pep rallies," I say sarcastically. "Who are we cheering on today? The middle-school football team? Soccer? Track and field? Do we have a new curling team?"

Gus laughs. "No curling. It's basketball," he says, peeking inside. "Actually, I think we're going to be pretty good this year. What are your thoughts on the team?"

"I think, yes," I say. "For sure. Way better."

I don't know if we were good last year or not. What has made them "pretty good" as opposed to last year? Is it a new player? A new coach? Are the opponents weaker and therefore our team becomes superior because the competition isn't as great?

"Emilia?"

"Hmm?"

"You don't know anything about the team, do you?"

"Nope."

Clarissa and Lacey stop right outside the gym. Clarissa waves at me. She's carrying her mellophone case.

"Emi Rose! I'm going to play!"

"Really? That's cool!"

"Right? Jennine is out sick and Mr. Carmichael said I get to jump in!"

"Awesome, Clarissa. Congratulations."

"You and Lacey should sit front row so you have the best view."

I glance behind Clarissa toward the rumbling gym.

"I'm really glad you're playing," I whisper, "but I don't want to be in there."

"Don't worry, Emi Rose," Clarissa says, putting her arm around me. "You'll come sit in the front row with Lacey and just make sure to keep eye contact with me the whole time. Okay?"

"Um," I say, looking around. "It's just so loud."

Clarissa has known I hate loud noises since the first time we had a fire drill in kindergarten. The alarm suddenly blared across the room in the middle of class. The teacher laid out the rules for what to do, but I just froze, holding my ears. It was like someone had poured ice water on my head. I started crying while kids dutifully followed the teacher's directions.

Clarissa took my hand and told me it would be okay. She was the only person I could see or hear. It was like she gave me focus in all that chaos.

"Do you trust me, Emi Rose?" Clarissa says, bringing me back to the pep rally.

"Yeah."

"The mellophone is one of the nicest-sounding instruments. If you just focus on me playing, you'll be all right."

"Hey, you can wear these," Gus adds, pulling out his headphones.

I take his headphones and offer a smile. "Thanks."

"Come on, Emi Rose, let's go!" I put the headphones on and stop just outside the entrance to look back at Gus as Clarissa takes my hand.

"Gus, come sit with Lacey and me."

Gus has taken out his video camera from his backpack and is inspecting it while Clarissa inspects him.

"I mean," Clarissa says in a singsong voice, "it's already pretty crowded in the front."

"Go ahead," he says. "I'm going to stand on the side where I can get better footage. You know, get some close-ups of your tuba playing, Clarissa."

"It's a mellophone, Gustavo."

Clarissa places the case on the floor and pulls out her horn. She shows it to Gus and then puts her lips to it. The mellophone makes a fart sound before settling into a note.

Lacey throws her head onto my shoulder, cracking up.

"Clarissa! You better show that horn some manners!"

"Shush it, Lacey Roberts!" Clarissa blurts. "I just needed to warm it up."

"Well, señoritas, I'll see you all inside."

"Bye, Gus," Lacey says.

"Hasta luego, Señor Gus," I say.

Clarissa just nods. The door swings open and Mr. Carmichael pops into the hall.

"Clarissa Anderson, what in the world are you doing standing around? Get on in there and get ready!"

"Right, sorry, Mr. Carmichael!"

Clarissa scurries inside, dragging her half-open case in one hand, her backpack falling down her arm, and the mellophone in the other hand.

"Bye! Sit up front!"

Lacey and I follow Gus inside.

"You can just sit with us, Gus. It's fine," Lacey says.

Chinh and Barry jump down from the bleachers and land by our side.

"Hey, can I be the boom mic operator again, G? You know, wear those headphones?"

"Not necessary," Gus says. "Plenty of sound in this place."

"Yeah, I know." Barry's eyes shift around. I can see he's uncomfortable.

"Hey," I say, handing him the headphones Gus gave me. "You wanna share these?"

"Huh? Nah, I'm okay. You use them, Emi."

"Hey, B," Gus interrupts. "Can you use your phone to film some extra shots? We'll put them all together in editing."

"Yup!" he says. Both jog over to where Mr. Carmichael is standing.

"Where'd G-money and Barry go?" Chinh missed the whole thing because he was on his phone.

"They're filming over there," I tell him.

Chinh nods. "Cool."

"Wanna sit with us?"

"Huh? Oh yeah, sure."

Chinh puts his phone in his pocket and walks over to the bench where Lacey has saved my seat.

"Oh hey, Chinh!" Lacey says.

"Yo."

I think I see Lacey's neck blush a little as Chinh sits. I scoot over and try to block out the sounds of the band practicing, the cheerleaders jumping and cheering, and Sammy the Screaming Eagle making the crowd get louder and louder with each "caw-caw, caw-caw!"

Clarissa is trying to get my attention. She gets scolded by Mr. Carmichael for not being in place as the Merryville Middle pep band initiates a messy jumble of drums, cymbals, and horns.

After the pep rally, Clarissa and Lacey head off together and I walk to homeroom to try to get this day over with. I need to pick up the books from my locker that I'll use for homework tonight. My phone is in there too. Mom usually texts me after school to make sure I take all of my work home with me. She must still be traveling.

There's a tap on my shoulder, and I know it's Gus before he says anything because I see his black Adidas with scuffed white tips.

"So, how was life in the front bleachers?" he asks. "Any new chisme to report? I need to keep up with school news."

I laugh. "Call it chisme or call it gossip, but definitely don't call it news."

"Touché," he says, showing me his camera screen. He

plays footage he took of the mascot. Sammy is supposed to be an eagle, but it's more like a bird whose face froze the second it heard something terrible.

"Did the headphones work?"

"Not really."

"Oh, sorry."

"I mean, they helped a little, but it was still disorienting. Seeing people jumping around quietly is almost as loud as noise. That's why I took them off."

"There was a moment when I thought my camera broke and I almost called you," he says. "But I fixed it."

I love solving problems and figuring out how to fix things. I think I get it from my mom. She's a computer genius.

On my ninth birthday, Abuela found an Easy-Bake Oven for sale online and bought it for me. I like eating sweets more than making them, so I decided to take the oven apart to see what was inside—what made it hot. It was an incandescent bulb, which is a pretty standard heat lamp and not very interesting. Anyway, I left a mess everywhere. Abuela didn't like that.

"Emilia?" Gus asks.

"Hmm?"

"¿Qué pasa in there?" He grins and points to my head.

I squint at him. Of all people, he already knows the answer to that.

Gus lets out one of his classic laughs and it echoes across the classroom. Kids stop and stare at him, but he doesn't care.

"What's so funny?" I ask.

"I love the way your mind works, Emilia Torres."

# CHAPTER FIVE

After school, Gus and I walk down Main Street toward the auto shop. I don't take the bus after school because Gus and I like to walk and hang out before we start our homework. He usually does his homework in Abuela's office and I go home to study with Mom. We tried studying together at the beginning of the year, but I kept getting distracted every time the compressor hissed to add air to a tire. Mom said I needed to be at home, where there was less going on. Abuela said I should learn to adapt.

"Necesita aprender estudiar así," Abuela said.

"She doesn't *need* to learn to study in an auto repair shop. She *needs* to learn to study. Period," Mom corrected.

Mom offered for Gus to come to the house to study, but his dad said he preferred for Gus to stay at the auto shop and work in Abuela's office.

Our mechanic-and-auto-body shop is the only one

of either in town. We do basic services like oil changes, air-filter replacements, and tire rotations. We also do cosmetic work like dent repair, paint jobs, and buffing. And if a car needs to be completely fixed up, we can do that, too. Abuela's office is in a little trailer overlooking each stall. I like it in there because Abuela has a wall-unit air conditioner that blasts icy air when it's hot and a heater that keeps the office warm like an oven when it gets cold.

"Have you given any thought to Mr. Richt's project?" I ask Gus as we cross Main Street.

"Sí," he says. "¡Algo con horror! Like the pep rally today."

"That *was* pretty terrifying."

"Seriously, though. I've been thinking about myths. It'd be cool to film a tour of all the places that are connected to cool myths in Merryville, ¿verdad?"

"Yeah," I say. "Do you know of any?"

"When I lived in Mobile, there was a myth about a mysterious creature called the Wolf Woman of Mobile, Alabama."

"Really?"

"Yeah," Gus says, getting closer. "Back in the 1970s, witnesses described a creature with the lower body of a wolf and the head of a woman. She was seen at night, stalking residents, but she never harmed anybody."

"No way!" I say, playfully shoving him.

"It's true! People reported sightings. It was in the paper and everything."

Gus has what teachers like to call "an active imagination." He stops kicking rocks down the sidewalk and turns to me, wide-eyed, wiggling his dark bushy eyebrows like he's just figured out something incredible.

"Can you imagine what monsters must be lurking in the shadows around this old town?" Gus gazes past the train tracks toward the edge of the woods. "So many possibilities yet to discover! And it could be a serious boost to the tourism in Merryville!"

"We hardly have tourism here."

"¡Exactamente!" Gus says, picking up another rock and bouncing it on his knee before kicking it off again. "I can help start it."

"¡Es una idea fantástica, Señor Gus!"

"¡Gracias, Señorita Emilia! I'm going to go to the library to research monster myths from this region."

This town seems perfect for legends. All the buildings

are super-old, like the brick shops with faded and flaking Coca-Cola signs plastered on the sides. Or Jimmy's Diner, which has been around since the sixties and barely seats twelve people.

Main Street can have an eerie vibe, depending on the time of day. There are lots of shops, some boarded up, like the one next to Eddy's Hardware.

The movie theater that used to only play one movie was refurbished about two years ago and turned into a multiplex that screens three movies.

There's the large clock tower that faces away from Main Street. It's like the people who built it didn't want to be reminded of the time while they walked down the street.

We get to the end of Main Street, past Delucci's, which has a sign in the window. I have to squint to read it. It says HELP WANTED: BILINGUAL WAITSTAFF.

"If they want a bilingual staff," I say, "shouldn't they include which language they want the staff to be bilingual in?"

Gus stops and thinks about what I just said.

"You make an excellent point."

We continue walking and it isn't long before we reach

the Methodist church, just across the street from the Catholic church, and walk right onto the gravel driveway of Toni's Auto Repair.

Gus's dad is in one of the stalls, wearing a mask while carefully painting the exterior of a car a dark blue-green color. He puts his paint gun down and lifts his mask when he sees us.

"¡Hola, chicos! ¿Cómo les fue hoy?"

"Bien, Apá," Gus replies.

"Gustavo, ¿quieres ayudarme después de terminar la tarea?"

"No, gracias," Gus says quickly, trying to avoid any further conversation of helping his dad paint the car.

Gus turns to me and whispers, "He's *always* trying to get me to paint a car with him, but I *always* find a way to stain my clothes. Even when I wear coveralls. It makes no sense."

"So you don't want to get car paint on you, but you don't care about fake blood when you're shooting a horror movie?"

"First of all, movie blood is just red food coloring inside little balloons hooked up to explosive devices called squibs. Totally different from toxic car paint that doesn't wash off in the laundry."

Abuela approaches from her office and waves at Gus.

"¿Qué tal, mi'jo?" she asks, standing next to me.

"Hola, Doña Aurelia," Gus responds.

It always sounds weird when Gus calls Abuela "Doña." He should just call her Aurelia or something. Gus says the "Doña" is simply out of respect. Personally, I think it's overkill.

Agustín, one of the mechanics, catches my eye as he fastens a trailer hitch and tow to an SUV. I don't know how he can even see what he's doing when his baseball cap practically touches his nose. He's a senior at Park View High School. He's been working afternoons and weekends at the shop since his sophomore year, except when it's soccer season. He got accepted to Georgia Tech a month ago, and his family threw a huge barbecue for him. We all went to his house to celebrate. I asked him what he wanted to study, and he said electrical engineering. Then out of earshot he whispered, "But if I'm being real, I'm excited to have *some* kind of social life outside this little town."

His sister, Amanda, is in tenth grade, and Agustín tells me she's a way better student than he ever was. His dad helps manage a flower farm in Blairsville and his mom works at a bakery in town.

"¡Hola, Agustín!" I wave.

"Hey! Emilia, how's life in middle school?"

"Fine," I tell him. "It feels like we have a pep rally every week."

"I hated pep rallies. Definitely happy to be done with those."

"Seriously."

"What's up, Gustavito?"

Gus thinks Agustín is the coolest guy in town. I have to admit, he's definitely the coolest teenager.

Agustín turns back to the hitch. He wipes his hands on his jeans and inspects his work.

"It's like he's not even trying to be awesome," Gus says, "but yet somehow, he is."

"Orestes," Abuela says to Gus's dad, "¿por qué no ayudas a Agustín?"

Gus's dad goes over to help Agustín tighten the hitch, but Agustín waves him off.

"I got it, Doña. Don't worry," he says. "I learned from the best." He bows at Abuela and smiles. He knows exactly what to say to her. Gus's dad slaps Agustín on the shoulder and heads back to the paint job.

I nod at Gus. "He *is* cool."

Just then, a bright blue Toyota Camry pulls into the garage. Abuela turns around and waves at the driver.

"Oh, hello there, Mary!" Abuela says, approaching the car.

It's Clarissa's mom. She steps out wearing a white V-neck and jeans, her brown hair in a tight ponytail that exposes streaks of blond at the ends. I tug at my own hair. My ponytail didn't really survive the day. I have loose strands along the sides that have frizzed into super-curls around my ears.

"Oh, Aurelia," she replies. "The engine light is on and I'm worried my car is going to break down! And I have to pick up Clarissa from band practice in fifteen minutes! Save me!"

"We'll have that checked out right away." Abuela motions for Gus's dad to join them.

"Orestes?" she calls out. "Can you please look at Mrs. Anderson's Camry? The check engine light is on."

"I'll take a look," Agustín says.

"Oh, that's sweet of you, young man, but I'm in a hurry and I need a professional."

Agustín stops short of the car and eyes Clarissa's mom. Before he says anything, Gus's dad has already arrived.

"Yo me encargo de este trabajo, mi'jo," Señor Orestes says to Agustín.

Agustín doesn't argue, but he watches Clarissa's mom for a moment. He lifts his cap, and his hair puffs out under the bridge of his hat before he heads to the stall to work on a Honda Civic that needs a new transmission.

Señor Orestes motions with his hands like he's turning a key.

"Oh, Mary," Abuela says. "Please hand me the keys so Orestes can get started."

"Sure thing," Mary says. "Oh, hey there, Emi Rose. How's it going?"

"Fine, thank you."

"Come, Mary," Abuela says, "let's go inside the office, where it's cooler." She leads Mary toward the air-conditioning.

Señor Orestes places a piece of paper over the Camry's floor mat before hopping into the driver's side, leaving one foot on the ground and one foot inside the car. He yanks a lever under the steering wheel and the hood pops open. While under the hood, he pulls out the dipstick and wipes it with a rag.

Gus looks just like his dad. Dark hair, bushy eyebrows,

kind eyes. Gus doesn't have a full mustache, but their smiles are identical. They extend from ear to ear and could easily light up the night sky.

Señor Orestes uses the little phone on the wall to call Abuela in the office to tell her the car just needs a simple oil change. It seems like Abuela gives him the okay, because he hangs up and starts the process.

In no time at all, the job is finished and Abuela comes out with Mary so she can collect her keys.

"You're a lifesaver, Aurelia—truly," Mary says.

"Not a problem," Abuela replies. "Oh, I forgot to ask how the job search is going."

"Let me tell you, it's getting harder and harder by the minute around here."

"I'm sure you'll find something," Abuela says.

"Seems like I'll have to take Spanish classes if I want a real job."

"Well, I'd be happy to get you a tutor. And Emilia can help Clarissa!"

"Oh, I don't have time for a tutor what with Clarissa's activities and church things. But thanks. Say hi to Toni when he gets back and tell Sue I need some help with my computer. I can't seem to get the screen to work right."

"I'll be sure to tell them," Abuela says, smiling so tightly, it's like someone glued her face like that.

"Oh! And please tell Toni we thank him for his service. Y'all should come over soon!"

Mary hops in her car and pulls away.

"Take care now, Mary!" Abuela waves both arms so much, it's like she's going to fly away.

Abuela checks her phone and shakes her head. "Esa mujer no quiere aprender nada." She tells me. "I've offered her Spanish lessons for over a year and she always has an excuse. "Entonces que no se queje."

"She does complain a lot about not finding work," I say. "Why doesn't she just accept your offer, Abuela?"

"Aye, mi'ja, quién sabe," she says. "Vamos, so you can finish your homework. Your father is already on his way! Let me get my things from the office and we'll go, okay?"

After Abuela is done, I say goodbye to Gus, Señor Orestes, and Agustín. Abuela pats Gus on the back then gives him the keys to the office. She tells him to make sure he locks the door when he leaves. Last week Gus forgot to put the keys in the lockbox and Abuela had to open late. She was not happy about asking customers to come back later. "Qué vergüenza," she said at the time.

Gus's dad takes him to the office and tells him to start his homework.

Abuela and I walk around to the back of the shop, down a narrow alleyway toward a metal door with a padlock on it. She punches in a code and pulls the latch, revealing our backyard. We walk up the little hill that overlooks the garage and where you can see the tops of the two-story buildings along Main Street. A train chugs in the distance.

We enter the house through the rear door and I flip on the lights in the kitchen. Abuela sets her bag down and starts rummaging through the refrigerator.

"I'm going to make your dad's favorite," she says. "Can you start la cafetera, Emilia?"

"Sí," I say, taking our Cuban coffeemaker from the stove and twisting it open to add a little water. I grab some Café Bustelo from the cupboard and pour the delicious roast into the filter. Cuban coffee has the most extraordinary smell in the world. Mom says, "It's the sweet aroma of our island and our ancestors."

"It's just café," Abuela always replies. "Café cubano."

The clock reads four thirty. In about an hour, my dad will finally be home. I wonder what my first words to him are going to be. Maybe I should have written a script.

# CHAPTER SIX

I perk up when the doorbell rings. A little beam of light illuminates the hall just outside the dining room. All the worries swirling around in my brain—what my first words should be, why he didn't call for so long or say anything about the videos I sent him, what it will feel like to finally see him after he's been gone for over eight months—completely disappear. And suddenly the perfect first word comes to me.

"Papi!" I say, jumping up. My dad grins from ear to ear when he sees me, and the entire house feels warm.

Papi's duffel bag thumps on the floor.

"Hey!"

My dad is home!

His wide shoulders press against his sharp uniform. His cover is tucked under his arm, exposing his reddish-brown hair, which is cropped tight. I run up to him, ready for him to lift me into a giant hug like he always does.

"Papi!" I repeat. When I reach him, he stops short of lifting me.

He takes both of his hands to the sides of my head then drops them behind my neck. He holds them there and stares.

"Hey there, Emilia," he says.

It makes my heart thump nervously and my head spin with what to do or say next.

"Antonio!" Abuela interrupts the moment as she walks in from the kitchen. Papi releases his hold and Abuela forces her way into a hug.

"Hola, Mami," he says, pulling away.

Abuela steps back and rubs my dad's back.

"¿Estás bien?" she asks.

"Yeah."

"Emilia made café con leche," she says. "It's all warmed up for you."

"Great," he says.

"And Abuela made pan con lechón!" I bounce around excitedly again.

My dad loves Abuela's sandwiches. So do I. The pork is garlicky and tangy and the bread has a paper-thin crust with a soft, flaky center. Abuela got the ingredients at Don Carlos's Grocery Latino on the other side of Merryville, near Park View Middle. You can't get Cuban bread anywhere else. Or Cuban coffee. You can't get mojo pork anywhere else either. At least not the way the butcher makes it at Don Carlos's store!

We walk from the entrance of the house to the dining room and sit down together. We're almost a complete family again. Only Mom is missing.

Abuela has already set a plate down with the pork sandwich and plantain chips at the head of the table, where my dad sits. Abuela pops up like she forgot something and then returns carrying a coffee cup on a saucer with a tiny spoon on the side. She places the coffee in front of the plate.

"Gracias, Mami," my dad tells Abuela. "So, how's school, Emilia?"

"Good," I say. "Where's your favorite place to go to in Merryville, Papi?"

He seems confused.

"Um, I don't know. Why do you ask?"

"I was just curious."

Papi meets Abuela's eyes and they both raise their brows like they're not sure what the heck I'm talking about. Abuela pats my shoulder and takes my dad's hand, the one that's not holding the Cuban sandwich. I start tapping my fingers on the table and Dad stares like he wants me to stop. I slow my finger tap to a halt and then look at both of them, unsure what to say.

"Emilia, why don't you tell your dad about school like he asked?"

They don't answer my question and I feel like asking it again, but then I think about my upcoming math test this Thursday.

"Mrs. Brennen asked me if I understood what constitutes a statistical question and I told her yes, but then she asked me to give an example and I said I didn't know."

"Okay . . ." my dad says, even more confused. "So, are you playing any sports this spring?"

"Sports?" Now it's my turn to be confused. "I don't play sports, Papi."

"Oh," he says. "I thought you wanted to try out for basketball or something."

"No," I say. "You and I played at the rec center, like, a year ago."

"Oh, that's right. I'm sorry, I didn't realize you weren't playing."

A piece of onion falls off my dad's sandwich. We all stare at it on the floor.

"So, I have to do a social studies project for Mr. Richt's class," I offer.

"I thought he was the coach of the JV football team."

"He is," I say. "And basketball and baseball and I think curling."

"Pretty sure Merryville has never had a curling team, Emilia."

"I know," I tell him. "I was joking."

My dad can usually pick up when I'm telling a joke, but it's like he forgot.

"Has Mom called?" he asks. There's a pause in his voice. His eyes shift to the living room.

"I think she's still flying, Papi," I tell him. "She said she had a lot of layovers."

"Oh okay," he says. "I'm sure she'll call when she's settled."

He takes one last bite of the pork sandwich and sips the last of his café con leche. He gets up and gives Abuela a peck on the cheek.

"Gracias, Mami," he says, then he walks over to me. "I'm going to take a little rest, Emilia. Maybe after we can catch up?"

My dad gives a sad kind of smile.

"Sure," I say.

He takes out his phone and turns it on. He waits for it to fully power up by the dining room door. I guess he doesn't find what he's looking for, because he puts it back in his pocket. Abuela heads in the opposite direction, back to the kitchen. I stay where I am.

My dad has been a Marine on active duty since I was four years old. Each time he left, my heart would drop into my knees. Then, when he returned, it was like he lifted my heart back into place and everything was right again. That's how it has always worked. It started with worry, but the relief would come once he was back.

I wonder when the relief will kick in. Maybe it will take longer now because he was away for more time.

My dad unbuttons his perfectly pressed shirt as he heads toward the stairs. He holds on to the railing, taking slow steps up the narrow staircase. I never understood why he didn't respond to any of the videos I sent him. I sent so many. Thirty, to be exact. I waited and waited but never got an answer. Even though he's home now, it still feels like I don't have an answer.

# CHAPTER SEVEN

The next day, after school, Gus and I decide to go straight to my backyard to sit on the hill overlooking the town. Trees cover the far side of Merryville and in the distance, I can see the train tracks.

"Everything seems so quiet and ordinary from here," I tell him.

"Sí, pero that's the thing about places like this. You can uncover secrets. I bet there are mythological creatures hiding in the woods over there. Lurking just outside the town."

Gus points his camera at me.

"Is Emilia Torres, explorer extraordinaire, going to uncover the mysteries of Merryville Woods before it's too late?"

"Why do I have to be the explorer?"

"Because I'm the filmmaker and you're the star."

"Can't you be the star *and* the filmmaker? And besides, isn't it supposed to be a *tourism* guide of Merryville?"

"Shock sells. Tourists would flock here like a bunch of birds after seeing my video about creepy creatures dwelling in the woods."

Gus drops his camera and points at my fingers. "I like that color," he says.

I stretch out my hand and look at my nails. "Baby blue," I say. "I wanted to add sparkles, but Abuela didn't let me."

"She's very traditional," he says.

"And controlling. I just wish she'd back off with her 'traditional' stuff once in a while."

"When does your mom get back?"

"Not soon enough."

Below the hill—just in the back lot of the auto shop— I see my dad.

"Can I use your camera, Gus?"

"Sure." He removes the strap from his shoulder and hands it to me. "Use the strap," he says. "So it doesn't fall."

"You got it."

I sling the strap over my shoulder and look through the eyepiece.

"See something?"

"It's my dad," I say.

"If you flip out the screen, you can zoom in," Gus says, pointing to the side of his camera.

"I thought you said that zaps the battery faster?"

"Well, sí, it does, pero you'll get to see what he's doing better with the zoom."

I open the little screen and can see my dad in the tiny frame.

"The zoom is here, right?"

"Sí," Gus says, pointing to the top of the camera where my hand is. "Ahí mismo."

I use my index finger to zoom in. "He's using the welder."

The camera shakes a little, so I use my other hand to steady it. My dad is working on a car. He takes a piece of sheet metal, places it on the workbench next to him, and measures the driver's-side doorframe. He grabs a smaller sheet and marks it up with a black Sharpie.

He puts on gloves, turns a knob on the welder and aims, then slides the shade down on his helmet so it covers his face. He positions the welding gun over his left hand like he's holding a pool stick, and carefully pulls the trigger.

"It's like we're spies," Gus whispers. "Like your father is a scientist forced to work on a secret space station designed to destroy planets."

"Isn't that a Star Wars story?"

"Possibly. Do you think J.J. Abrams will hire us to direct one?"

"One what?" I reply while still focused on my dad.

Brilliant blue sparks shoot up into the sky like they're trying to jump over the fence. The sound of metal cracking tickles my heart. It doesn't bother me like other loud noises. There is unity in the *crack-crack-crack* of the welding gun fusing metal. I know these sounds. I've grown up with them. They remind me of home. My dad releases the gun and moves to another spot.

"To direct a Star Wars movie," Gus says. "You could direct one and I could direct another. And they can link up somehow, but you won't find out until after the title credits."

"I don't know," I say. "Maybe. Look how the sparks fly around whenever he squeezes the trigger on the welding gun. It's like they're dancing."

"My tita dances like that," Gus says. "She's eighty but moves around like she's got firecrackers in her pantalones."

79

*Pop-pop-pop* echoes throughout the back lot. Dad moves the welding gun in circular motions, connecting the smaller piece of sheet metal to the larger one. When he's done, he takes off his helmet and walks the newly connected pieces to the doorframe. It doesn't seem to fit the right way. Papi rubs the top of his head and shakes it in frustration.

He digs around like he's trying to find something, then turns back to the welder and shuts it off. He leaves his helmet and gloves on the workbench and checks his phone.

"I wonder what he's working on back there all alone." I pan the camera to the front hood of the car. I zoom in even more on a shiny emblem—a snake with letters and numbers under it. "What kind of car is that?"

"No sé," Gus says.

Just then, Abuela steps through the gates. I zoom out. She marches up the hill, taking long strides.

"I think this is the end of our spy film," Gus says.

I move the camera up and down in agreement.

Abuela stands a few inches away from us and waits until we acknowledge her.

"I have an idea, mi'ja," she says, planting her foot like

she's squished a bug into the dirt. "Let's take your father out to dinner to celebrate his return."

Abuela doesn't wait for me to agree. She just hands the shop keys to Gus. "Can you please lock up, mi'jo?"

"Sí," he replies. We exchange shrugs. The camera goes back around his shoulder as he starts down the hill.

Meanwhile, Abuela spots my dad working in the back lot. She calls out his name in full volume.

"Antonio!"

Dad keeps welding. Abuela yells again and this time I cover my ears.

"Antonio!"

Dad has stopped welding, but he still doesn't reply. Abuela tries one more time.

"Antonio!"

"What?" he barks, throwing a piece of sheet metal on the floor. He slams the welding gun on the workbench and lifts his helmet up in one frustrated motion. Abuela has her hands on her hips and I'm crouched in a ball, covering my ears. My dad and I make eye contact, but I quickly turn away.

"Dinner out tonight!" Abuela screams.

"Okay, fine," he says, pulling down his helmet again to

cover his face. He shakes his head as he grabs the welding gun, sending a few more *crack-crack-crack*s into the sky.

"We'll go wherever you want to go, Antonio!"

Abuela waits for a response, but my dad doesn't answer.

"He must be jet-lagged from so much travel," she says. "Where do you think he'll want to eat?"

"Delucci's?"

"¡Sí! Your papi loves that place. Excellent choice!"

"Abuela?" I ask. "I have some math homework I need to finish."

"Finish it now and I'll call and make a reservation for six."

"Since when do we eat at six?"

"Your papi said he usually eats at six."

"Um . . ." I mumble, getting up and following Abuela. He's never wanted to eat this early. "Abuela, that will only give me an hour and a half to do my homework."

"You get out of school at three fifteen," she says. "What have you been doing since then? Just sitting in the backyard with Gustavo, I see."

"We were talking about our social studies project."

I never walk directly to the auto shop after school. Abuela knows that. We take our time and always make it by around four, when we each go off to do our homework.

"Emilia?"

"Hmm?"

"Start now and finish the rest of your homework after dinner," Abuela says, heading inside the house. I'm not far behind her.

"Abuela?"

She pauses. "¿Sí?"

"I might need a little help with my math," I say. I feel guilty for asking. It seems like Abuela always has something better to do than explaining subjects I don't get. Subjects I *should* get. Mom tells me to not be afraid to ask. I have to at least *try* to ask questions when I don't know the answer.

Abuela nods. "Bueno," she says, "I think it's a good opportunity to ask your papi. I'll text him."

I work for about twenty minutes before my dad comes home. He tosses his phone on the counter and paces around the kitchen. He must have finished whatever he was working on or maybe Abuela asked him to cut out early to get ready for dinner. Judging by the way he looked at his phone just now—like he wanted to throw it in the garbage—it was probably the second reason. That's one thing Mom and Abuela have in common—both text, like, a thousand times until you answer.

In the dining room, I take out my homework and spread it across the table. I wonder if Mom is going to text. She knows I start my homework around this time. I can do my homework by myself, but it helps when she's around. At least to point me in the right direction. I check my screen a few times, like maybe Mom can see me through the phone.

The numbers on my math sheets make me remember the emblem on the car my dad was working on. I didn't recognize it, but it seemed like some kind of sports car.

*Tap-tap-tap.*

It's Abuela knocking on the glass tabletop.

My dad walks through the dining room to the living room, mumbling hello as he passes. He turns on the TV to the fishing channel. The fisherman is reeling in something that must be huge. The guy makes lots of "woo-hoo!" sounds. I guess he's excited.

Just as the fisherman catches a big fish, my phone buzzes across the table. It's Mom!

"Hey, mi amor!"

"Hi, Mom! How's San Francisco?"

"Good! Lots of meetings. I'm taking a break now, though. Homework time?"

"Yes!"

"What's on the agenda for math today?"

"I have my worksheets right here. Video call?"

Before I can wait for an answer, Mom's face appears on my screen. Her hair is up in a messy bun, and she's wearing eyeliner and pink lipstick that pops against her skin.

"You look so pretty, Mom."

"Thank you, mi amor. I love this color. It's called Blushing Caribbean Sunset. It's from a company run by two colombianas from Barranquilla."

"I love it. Can I borrow some when you're back?"

"¡Claro! Want to get started?"

"Let's do this."

We've caught my dad's attention and Mom notices.

"Is that Papi over there?"

"Yeah," I say.

"T! What's up, honey?"

"Hey," my dad says without moving. "How is it going over there?"

"Good," Mom replies. I aim my phone at the living room. "I'll call you after I work with Emilia."

Dad seems to smile as she says this. It's a soft smile. I almost miss it because it disappears as soon as it starts. I turn the phone back to me.

"How's Papi doing?" Mom asks, concerned.

"I don't know," I say. "He seems kind of lonely."

"He's jet-lagged," Abuela interjects, popping into the frame behind me.

"Hey, Aurelia. ¿Qué tal?"

"Bien," Abuela says. "Everybody here is fine. Antonio was about to help Emilia with homework."

"¿No me digas? Cool!"

Mom asks me to show her my math sheet. It's like she didn't even bother to consider what Abuela offered.

She and I begin to go over some problems while Abuela watches.

"Mi amor," Mom says. "What are you looking at?"

"Hmm?"

"You're not paying attention."

It's the TV. The fisherman is having a good fishing day. "Yes, I am."

"Aurelia," Mom says. "Can you ask Toni to turn off the TV?"

"I was just going to tell him that," Abuela says. She

mutes the TV just as the guy pulls another large fish out of the water. "Antonio, Emilia needs a little help with her homework."

My dad doesn't move his head. Only his eyes.

"Isn't Sue helping her?"

"Sí, pero she's going to get off the phone soon and then you can help la niña before we go to dinner."

She grabs the remote and turns off the TV while my dad watches me curiously. "Susanna, I think Antonio can help out so you can get back to work."

Mom checks her watch. "I can work with her through these math sheets and then Toni can help her with the rest of the stuff."

Mom and I go through statistics problems for about thirty minutes before she has to go.

"I love you with all my heart, sweetie."

"Love you too, Mom."

"I'll call Mrs. Jenkins to make sure they send me your homework."

"Mom, I don't need you to call Mrs. Jenkins. You're only gone for a few days."

"But it's long enough to fall behind, mi amor. And I love helping my favorite girl."

"Fine." I say goodbye and get a falling-in-quicksand feeling. My dad takes a seat next to me. Abuela pats him on the shoulder.

"I'll let you two study for a little bit."

She heads upstairs to her room and leaves us to stare at each other.

"So . . ." Dad says.

"I'm okay, Papi," I tell him. "You can watch fishing if you want."

"It's fine," he says, but I'm not convinced. He sounds like he doesn't want to be here. "Do you understand this stuff?"

That's a question I've been asked in one way or another, my entire life. When I was in third grade, my teacher, Ms. Gretchen, was worried that I wasn't learning enough to show "mastery of grade-level content" to pass to the fourth grade. The thing is, I knew more than I was supposed to know. I could fix the computer when Abuela did something to it. I could multiply in my head. I could put two-thousand-piece puzzles together. I even changed my first tire when I was nine!

"Do you have a lot of homework?" my dad asks.

"Not too much," I tell him.

"Abuela says that if you're doing your homework, the TV should be off," he says. "Is that true?"

I nod. I focus on my dad's really short hair. There is a little red stubble appearing on his cheeks.

"So, what are you studying?" he asks.

I take out more of my folders, binders, and my agenda and scatter everything all over the dining room table.

I plop my workbook on top of it all to look through the language arts pages I have to complete tonight.

"Pretty messy on that table," he says. "If you were in my unit, we would've had to wake up at 0300 and run ten miles in the freezing cold 'cause of that mess."

I must look worried, because he shuffles around, trying to explain himself.

"That was a joke," he says.

We're both missing each other's laugh tracks.

"Sorry," I respond. "I usually put my papers everywhere and then little by little I organize what needs to go where."

"Hmm," he says. "Do you still like puzzles?"

"Yeah," I say. "I still do."

"Cool," he says. "Maybe you can think of all these papers like a puzzle. Put them together so they're neat and make sense."

"Yeah," I say. Papi's hand is on the table. He's wearing his wedding ring.

*Tap-tap-tap. Tap. Tap.*

"Emilia." Abuela reappears in the room. She hovers over Papi's shoulder. I get the urge to talk to Mom again, but she said she had to go. She's exactly two thousand, four hundred, and eighty-six point two miles away if you go from Atlanta to the Golden Gate Bridge. I Google Mapped it.

"I'm not sure she understands the homework," Papi says, getting up.

It's not that I don't understand. I just need to be able to talk about the problem out loud.

"Emilia," Abuela says, putting her arm on me. "Do you need to stand up?"

"Yeah, maybe," I say. I stretch while looking at the little short stories and multiple-choice questions that follow.

"That's not right," he says. "None of these answers are correct."

My dad paces. He's frustrated. I can tell because he keeps rubbing the stubble on the side of his head just above his ears.

"I hope you're getting good grades," he says. "Don't want you falling behind."

"I'm not!" I bark.

"Emilia, no le hables así a tu papá."

I don't usually talk to anyone like this, especially my family, but something about Dad hovering and questioning my work wakes up my anger for an instant.

I grab my eraser and rub out the choice I made so hard, it practically rips the paper. I sweep away all the tiny pieces of rubber and pick up my pencil to underline the sentences in the story. I write *thesis statement* in bold and then skim the story before looking back at the question-and-answer section.

"So," I start to explain out loud, without looking back at him. "Because the story began with James Oglethorpe coming to Georgia, then the answer is C. And here it says he established trade . . ."

My dad watches me work. I use the pencil to make dark circles around my choices. "The answer is B on question two and D on question six. Those are the correct answers."

Abuela pats me on the back. Papi's eyes move from my language arts sheet to me.

"You see?" Abuela says. "When you focus, you get the answer."

It wasn't focus that got the answer. It was anger. Frustration. Abuela doesn't get it. It's not that easy.

She leaves me and my dad alone at the table again. Papi

eyes the pile of work I have spread out, and I think the mess makes him nervous. He starts gathering the papers into one pile. Once he realizes he can't organize it all for me, he decides to leave.

"I'm going to grab something to eat," he says.

Papi returns with a Coke and a plate of potato chips with cheese sauce. He stands next to me, crunching on the ruffled chips. A little cheese sauce falls on his chin. Why is he eating before dinner?

"Your room is a little messy too," he says. "Please tidy it up before we go."

Dad walks into the living room and plops down on the sofa. He takes a long drink of his Coke and finishes it in one gulp.

I don't really know what else to do, so I study the statistics homework sheet I completed with Mom. We're supposed to explore and become familiar with what available data we have in order to find meaning in the samples. I can't seem to find meaning in any of the data my dad is giving me.

When I'm done with my homework, I go upstairs to my room and shove as much stuff into my closet as I can. It doesn't quite look clean. I decide to take everything out again and clean up for real.

As I fold a pile of clothes, I start to get mad again. It feels like Dad has forgotten who I am. I tried to tell him on my videos, so he wouldn't forget. I sent *thirty* and he didn't respond to any of them. Not one. Over the last year, we would talk briefly on the phone, but he never mentioned having received them. I know being away from us wasn't easy, so on top of being mad, I also feel kind of guilty.

I don't like having so many feelings sloshing around inside me. I'm starting to feel like the lemon–Coke bottle rocket again.

Abuela catches me sitting inside my closet. She steps over a few LEGO boxes I put out to give away. I've already assembled and reassembled every Star Wars, Harry Potter, and Marvel *and* DC Comic LEGO I've ever received. Dad got me the *Death Star* a few years ago, and I put it together by myself in three days. I haven't touched them lately, though.

"Tu papi prefiere quedarse en casa," Abuela says.

"What? Why did he change his mind about dinner?"

"I think he's still a little tired," she says. "It'll take a few days. I told him not to fill up on comida basura like chips and soda before dinner."

Abuela starts to leave, but I stop her before she does.

"Oh, Abuela?"

"¿Sí?"

"You can give those to the church," I tell her, pointing to the boxes of LEGOs.

"Your LEGOs?"

"Yeah."

"Okay," she replies. "I can take them to the church this Sunday. You and your father can help out."

"Sure," I say.

Abuela leaves and I start piling the LEGOs neatly in a corner. When I'm done cleaning my room, I go outside to watch the sun set over the town. It's the time of day when things don't feel so rushed. When I can just be quiet with my thoughts.

I'm surprised to find my dad out back, sitting on the porch swing. He's staring over the grassy hill, barely moving a muscle. I go to say hello and notice that his eyes are only slightly open, but he doesn't respond to me as I get closer. I know he's not awake. I don't want to wake him, so I just smile, hoping he is having a nice dream. It seems like maybe he needs one.

# CHAPTER EIGHT

I had to stay after school to speak with Mrs. Jenkins, who asked about my homework and if I needed any help. "No, thank you," I told her, but she still said she wanted to send a note to my teachers.

I know Mom called her to make sure I didn't forget anything. I felt my throat dry up and my cheeks burn. "I told my mom that she didn't have to say anything to you."

"Emilia, I'm here for any additional support you need. Anything. Oh, and let's talk about the electives for next year."

I promised her I would have an answer at our next meeting so she would let me go.

When I arrive at the library, Gus is already waiting for me outside. He's filming a redbrick building. He pans the camera to me when he notices I'm next to him.

"I really like this place," he says.

The library is an old converted schoolhouse with enormous wooden beams, one huge window, and carpeting that appears to have been stepped on for years. The whole room smells like old books. It's kind of stuffy and mildewy, but not in the lonely, nobody-lives-here way. There's something about the smell that feels like it's whispering secrets to you. Like there's something to be discovered within its musty old walls if you just listen.

I browse the local history section while Gus reads a book called *Myths and Legends of the American South*.

"There are chapters on different regions!" he says, a little too loudly. I check to see if the librarian is going to shush us.

It feels like there is a chorus of stories about to sing out from these books at any moment, and I get to choose the songs to listen to. The librarian comes over and asks if I need any help.

"I'm okay," I tell her, but she must see the look on my face because she asks me more questions.

"Are you in Mr. Richt's sixth-grade social studies class?" she asks.

"Yes," I tell her.

"A few of your classmates have come in this week asking for information for a project y'all are doing. My name is Mrs. Becker," she says. "But you can call me Liz. Liz the Librarian!"

Mrs. Liz lets out a hearty laugh and stops abruptly. She puts her finger to her lips, hushing herself even though the library is mostly empty.

"Whoops," she says.

I laugh a little.

"Imagine a librarian hushing herself in her own library!"

I wonder why I haven't seen Mrs. Liz around. I know a lot of people because everyone needs an oil change at some point, and I've spent most of my life in Abuela's auto shop. Maybe Mrs. Liz doesn't drive. There was a bike locked out front.

"Well, I can help you out," Mrs. Liz says. "What's your name, dear?"

"Emilia," I tell her.

"Okay, Emilia," she says. "What are you looking to research?"

I tell her that I don't have a project topic yet.

"Well," she says, "let's see. The project is supposed to introduce an imaginary visitor to Merryville, right? To our places of interest."

"Right. But everyone around here already knows Merryville, so that's hard."

"Well, what's your favorite thing to do in town?" Mrs. Liz asks.

I think.

"Café con leche. I drink it every morning with my mom before school. That's when we talk." My heart aches a bit when I mention Mami.

"What else?"

"My dad just came back from service and my abuela and I made him a special sandwich to welcome him home. So, also that sandwich. But a visitor can't just go to my house to eat a sandwich. That would be a boring trip."

"If you invite them, it wouldn't! But it might get a little tiresome having all those people over at your house, huh?"

"Yeah."

"So, what makes that sandwich so special? Where can a visitor get a sandwich like the one your grandma made for your daddy?"

"Well," I start, "it's got a kind of pork you can only buy in one store across town. It's where we get our café, too."

"It sounds like that grocery store has some unique ingredients that might interest tourists, don't you think?"

I'm not sure what we'd do if Don Carlos's Grocery Latino didn't exist. Abuela would probably make us move!

"I think I'm going to add Don Carlos's Grocery Latino as the first stop on my tour," I tell Mrs. Liz.

"That's great! What do you think you'll write about it?"

This is a tough question. Disney World is a place for tourists. I see Don Carlos every week, but I never thought of his place as a destination. Sometimes we eat tacos in the little Mexican restaurant in the back of the store. Don Carlos came to my First Communion and he's been to every birthday party since I can remember. Don Felix, Don Carlos's butcher, is the one who delivers the pierna we eat on Nochebuena. He has dinner with us every year because Abuela insists he not eat alone on Christmas Eve.

"I think I'll talk to Don Carlos about his story," I say. "Like why he opened a store in Merryville and when he opened it. Stuff like that. I think it could be interesting for visitors to learn about Don Carlos while munching on garlicky pork sandwiches!"

"You're making me hungry just thinking about it! It sounds like you have a plan. Now, just let me know if I can help with anything else. I'll be over by the microfilm machine trying to fix it. It's been getting a workout this week!"

Mrs. Liz is easy to talk to. It doesn't seem like she's trying to help because she thinks you don't know the answer. Or because she gets impatient when you take long to come up with an answer yourself.

Mrs. Liz turns to leave, and I follow her. I want to know what a microfilm machine is and why it's broken.

"Is it for the Internet?" I ask.

I don't think Mrs. Liz knew I was behind her because she jumps a little.

"Oh goodness! Gave me a fright. No, honey." She stops at a bulky machine that reminds me of a computer from the old days. Big and clunky with a ton of knobs and dials and a screen that's more like the glass on a really large microwave door than a computer.

"It's analog," Mrs. Liz says proudly.

She flips a switch and the machine hums to life. Then she fiddles with a few buttons, and an old newspaper article about Georgia paper production in the early 1900s pops up on the screen.

"You think of a date and I can check in our catalog to see if we have a newspaper clipping on microfilm from that date," she says. "You just insert the film into this slot here and the machine will project the article onto this screen."

"That's really cool," I tell her. "So, what's wrong with it?"

"Oh, it just keeps acting up is all." Mrs. Liz pauses for a moment. "I don't really know what's wrong."

I ask Mrs. Liz if I can take a look.

"Be my guest," she says.

I peek behind the machine and inspect the screen.

"I'm going to need some tools," I tell her. I show her the panel behind the monitor. "There might be a blown fuse that needs replacing."

"You're the expert," she says.

I ask her if there is a mechanics section in the library.

"We have a technology section over there," she says, pointing. "I'll check the system to see if there are any books on microfilm machines."

While she does that, I walk over to the technology section.

"Don't know why I didn't think of that first! You're one smart cookie, Emilia."

The tech section has a few books on computers. A couple of coding books, a few on software, one on sewing. I catch a title between *Computing Made Simple* and *The History of the Paper Mill*. I pull out a book and read the cover: *The Totally Essential Shelby Mustang Guide 1965–1970*. The car on it is just like the car my dad was working on yesterday.

I open to the first chapter and read a few sentences, then I look at the diagrams. The car in the picture is almost identical, except my dad's is a rusty olive-green color and this one is shiny and silver. Both have the same emblem on the hood and on the side of the car. A snake in attack mode, and silver block letters and numbers just below that say GT 350. I close the book and ask Mrs. Liz if I can take it home.

"Of course!" she says. "I'll swipe your library card and you'll be all set."

"Oh, I don't have a library card. Where do I get one?"

"Well, we just need proof of where you live. That's it!"

"So, I can't take this book without a card?"

"I'm afraid not," Mrs. Liz says. "But let's find a solution. You can call your momma and she can confirm the address and we'll get you started. How's that sound?"

I pick up my phone. Mom won't be calling me for at least another thirty-five minutes. I don't feel like waiting that long.

"My mom is out of town," I say.

Gus wanders over and shows me another book. He opens to a specific page and points to a strange-looking creature emerging from a river surrounded by trees.

"The Etowah River Monster!" he says, again a little too loudly. "The legend is that a snakelike creature with fins that're kind of like the Loch Ness Monster's swims along the Etowah River even to this day! Only thing is, there isn't any documentation that it's anywhere near Lake Arrowhead or the small creeks that border parts of Merryville."

"Interesting," I say. "Hey, do you have a library card?"

"Sí, ¿por qué?"

"I want to check out this book."

"Okay," he says. "Mrs. Liz, please put Señorita Emilia's book on my tab."

"I can pay you back."

Gus and Mrs. Liz laugh.

"It's a library," Gus says. "Books and information are free here."

"That's so cool," I say, but inside I'm all tangled wiring. I didn't know that about libraries. My mom downloads audiobooks for me and buys hard copies online.

"Gustavo will check out the book for you and next time

you'll get to check out a book with your brand-new library card."

"Great," I say. Just then, I think about something that might help both me and Gus with our projects. "Hey, doesn't Don Carlos have a chupacabra piñata at the store? Maybe you can use it as a prop."

"He does! But I'd rather catch one in action. Do you think there are chupacabras in Merryville?"

"I don't know. Maybe."

"What's a chu-pa-cab-ra?" Mrs. Liz asks.

"It's a goat-eating creature that stalks around farms," Gus tells her.

"Oh my!" Mrs. Liz shouts. "That's terrifying. And we have lots of farms around these parts!"

Mrs. Liz seems genuinely frightened. She shifts around uncomfortably as if a chupacabra will pop out at any moment.

"It's a myth, Mrs. Liz," I tell her. "Myths aren't real."

"You're right," she says. "Tell me more about Don Carlos's grocery store. I only moved here from Decatur a few months ago, but I haven't seen it."

I tell her the store sells all kinds of things, like sweets from Venezuela and Colombia. Don Carlos is from

104

Venezuela. He sells onions and peppers and eggs and stuff like that, too. There's a carnicería with all kinds of meats in a display case. It's different from the other butcher shop in town because Don Carlos sells chorizo, which is a little spicier than regular sausage.

"Emilia?"

"Hmm?"

"You're going to start your tour at Don Carlos's?" Gus asks.

"I think so," I say. "What do you think?"

"Excellent choice," he says. "Are you just doing one stop, or will you go somewhere else, too?"

"I don't know," I tell him. "Maybe I'll add the library?"

"That's real sweet of you, Emilia," Mrs. Liz says.

"I like this place," I tell her, looking around. "It feels like people should visit. Plus, you can get something if you come."

"What's that?"

"Information."

Mrs. Liz nods and gives me a pat. "Thanks for promoting your local library, Emilia!"

"Hey, maybe we can help each other with our projects?" Gus offers.

"It would be cool if you could go with me to Don

Carlos's. And I'll totally help you with your film!"

"¡Por supuesto!" Gus replies. "It's going to be the first-ever horror film shot entirely in Merryville!"

"Wait, it has to be a tourism guide."

"Well, yes, pero adding a little horror is sure to attract visitors. Other cities have haunted tours. Why can't we?"

"You're right. So, you'll cover the Etowah River Monster?"

"Nah," Gus says. "The Etowah River is too far away. But some of these creeks around Merryville lead to Arrowhead Lake. There's bound to be a giant platypus or something."

"A platypus? That's not scary at all."

"Those things have spurs on the backs of their feet that emit poison. If it whacks you, you're going to be in agony for days."

"That does sound painful," I tell him. "We'll go check out your mutant platypus after visiting Don Carlos's grocery store tomorrow. Okay?"

We seal the deal with our special handshake. Gus checks out a few books, including the one about the Shelby, and we both thank Mrs. Liz.

Outside, Gus can't stop talking about the project. "You know, we're coming up on magic hour. I'm going to film a few quick exterior shots of the town right now. Wanna come?"

I study the book in my hand and shake my head.

"You go ahead. I'm going to go to the shop."

"Okay," Gus says. "See you later, Señorita Emilia."

"Good day, good sir," I say, bowing.

"Such a chivalrous lady," he says. "Hasta luego."

"You're going to trip and fall!" I tell him as he continues bowing and walking backward. He straightens up and makes a scary face before he turns around and heads in the opposite direction.

# CHAPTER NINE

I get to the auto shop and Señor Orestes tells me that my dad is out back again, working on the car. I can see a slight look of concern on his face.

Señor Orestes and my dad have always gotten along. They both share a love of soccer, though they have serious disagreements about whose club is better. Gus's family is from Guadalajara, Mexico. His dad is a Chivas *fanatic*. That's the Guadalajara team.

"Bah!" my dad said once, during a disagreement with Gus's dad at our house. "No way they're better!"

"Never been downgraded to second tier," Señor Orestes said, "*and* the winningest record. *And* homegrown talent."

"Here he goes," my dad said, waiting for Gus's dad to list all the great international players.

"Carlos Vela, Marco Fabián. Omar Bravo!"

"Oh boy," I remember Gus saying. "Don't get my dad started on Omar Bravo."

"All-time leading soccer star, played at Deportivo de la Coruña in Galicia, played for Kansas City MLS team! Homegrown talent, from where, hijo?" Señor Orestes pointed to Gus like a wizard casting a really intense spell.

"Guadalajara."

"¡Órale!"

Gus's dad lived in Alabama from the time he was a teenager. His parents moved to the States in the eighties and worked in the chicken plants. When he was going to start college, his parents got sick and he had to leave school. He had a knack for painting and wound up working at paint and auto body shops most of his life.

"He could've been a painter," Gus said. "Like, a legit artist."

"I've seen his work," I told him. "He's amazing."

Most of Gus's aunts and uncles live in Mexico now. They visit family in Guadalajara every year, but Gus tells me that his dad never wanted to move back.

"Me gusta este país," he said, referring to the United States. "And I found your mother here."

"They're so corny," Gus said. "My dad calls my mom 'la paloma,' then sings 'cucurucucú, paloma' to her any chance he gets."

"That's sweet."

"Not when your dad sounds more like a crow than a dove."

"You should go talk to your dad, mi'ja," Señor Orestes says. "Parece que lo necesita."

"What do I talk to him about?"

"You'll think of something," he says. "And when he *does* talk, listen."

I nod.

Like Señor Orestes said, my dad is in the back lot, working by himself. He's doing the same thing still—trying to fit the doorframe and sheet metal together.

Dust kicks up from my feet as I walk along the gravel. I set my backpack down next to an old tractor tire and take the book I checked out from the library. When I look up, Papi's moving the sheet metal to the workbench. He clamps down the metal and switches on the welder. He moves to the supply shed right next to me.

"Oh, hey, Emilia," he says. "Back from school?"

"Library."

"Good day?" He digs around in the shed. After a few minutes he emerges with a pair of tools I don't recognize.

"I think I chose my tour sites," I tell him.

"What's that now?"

"My social studies project topic. It's a tourism guide for Merryville."

"Great," he says, walking back to the workbench like he's not really listening.

"Hey, Papi?" I try to think of a memory that might make him smile. Or at least listen.

He turns his head, which is fitted with a welding helmet, visor up, so I can see his stubbly face. "Yeah?"

"You remember when I was in third grade, at the school assembly, and the principal called me up to the stage and said someone special was there to see me?"

I get closer, the book clutched to my chest.

"Well," I continue, "when I turned around, you were there, standing in your blue coat and white pants and you were smiling from ear to ear. I didn't even wait for the principal to stop talking. I ran as fast as I could and jumped into your arms and you swung me around and around."

Papi nods but doesn't say anything. He offers the

saddest smile I've ever seen. His body kind of sags like the way a tractor tire slowly deflates when you let the air out of it.

"That was the best time I've ever had at a school assembly, Papi," I say. I hand him the book.

He takes it and inspects.

"You like the Shelby?" he asks, looking at the book instead of at me.

"Yeah," I tell him. "But it's pretty broken-down."

"Just needs some TLC, that's all."

"Is it going to stay that color or are you going to paint it silver like the one on the book cover?"

My dad's face relaxes.

"You don't like it?"

"It's the color of a dirty olive."

He laughs. "Don't hate on the Green Hornet! It's a 1968 Shelby Mustang. Freshest car ever."

"I like the snake on the side."

Papi nods. "The cobra is pretty sick." He reads a page in the book I gave him. "You know, if you wanna stick around and help, you can. If you want to."

I feel a sudden rush of excitement. My dad wants me to help him. Gus's dad was right: I *did* think of something.

"You up for it?"

"Yes," I say quietly, but inside I might as well be one hundred and forty amps of electricity hitting metal.

"Cool," he says, handing me his gloves. "Take these. I'll go get another pair."

Papi hands me a dead blow hammer, which is safer than a regular hammer, and shows me how to strike the metal to bend it the way we want. He puts his arm around my shoulders. "You remember that tire we patched a few years ago?"

Of course I remember. Every detail, actually.

I follow my dad to the shed to get more supplies. He hands me small tools to carry back to the workbench. It's like we're flying a plane and I'm his copilot.

"So, Papi, how was your last deployment?" I ask. The question feels strange, but the time feels right. Especially because I really want to know.

"Fine," is all he says. He doesn't even look up from what he's doing.

"Were you in the mountains?" We move back to the car and I hand him a black Sharpie so he can mark it up.

"We're going to do a few butt welds here to fit the twenty-gauge into the doorframe. But first we have to get rid of the splotchy paint around the car. Some fool tried to paint it white. See this here?"

He shows me a few spots on the Hornet. He says he's been sanding the car down to bring it back to its original green.

"It still has some remnants of the original color. But we have to sand it down now and then we'll repaint. Sound good?"

"Oh okay," I say, trying to keep up.

He takes out two sets of goggles and two sets of masks that go over your mouth and nose. He fastens the mask on himself to show me how. When I put on mine, I can feel my own breath bouncing back at me. We lower our goggles and get close to the car. Papi shows me how to rub the paint off the hood using an electric sander.

The sound reminds me of the propeller from the radio-controlled airplane he got me for Christmas one year. We flew it from the hill in the backyard and it ended up soaring across the lawn, straight over the auto shop, and into a beech tree. The hum of the airplane sounded like a bumblebee. Bumblebees aren't dangerous. They just float and buzz around, eating nectar and pollinating stuff. They don't even sting unless you mess with them. That's what the sander sounds like. A giant bumblebee.

"When your eyes are focused on sanding the metal," my dad says in a muffled voice through his mask, "it becomes the only thing you see or hear other than your teammate next to you. For example, I know *you're* here, but I can't tell you what Orestes is doing in the stall out front."

I think about what Gus's dad told me, and just listen.

"And if I turn around to look at what he's doing, or if I call Abuela to see where she's at, then I could lose focus on this job, you see?"

"Yeah!" I say at full volume.

"Then mistakes can happen," he says. He turns toward the street and pushes the sander against the door. The screech blasts my ear and makes me jump back.

"You see?" he asks, taking the sander off the hood. He puts it on the workbench, pulls down his mask, and slides the goggles on top of his head. "You turn away from what you need to do, and you can hurt your teammate."

I lift my goggles too, and pull down my mask. Papi brushes off some of the leftover paint chips with his gloves. There's a slight burned smell in the air.

"You all right?" Papi asks, picking up the sander again.

"Yeah."

We're both quiet for a moment as the sander rests peacefully on the workbench.

"We had tower guard at some point during the night," he says out of the blue. "I'd sit there in the dark, four hours some nights, trying to communicate with the local military that shared the tower with us."

"Oh," I say. He's talking about his deployment. I try my best to act casual and not interrupt him so he'll keep talking.

"Got pretty close with some of those fellas. Had green tea and flatbread most nights. I always wanted the last shift. The one right before breakfast. I'd be up in that tower at three in the morning just looking out into the expanse."

"Why did you like that time of day, Papi?"

"I wanted to be awake at the quietest, darkest moment."

Dad stops. It seems like that's all he's going to say, so I work up the courage to ask him another question. My heart beats fast as I open my mouth.

"Was it cold?"

"Yeah, it got pretty cold up there. Hey, let's move over to the quarter panel and inspect."

116

And just like that, I know it's over.

"Okay," I say, feeling deflated.

After about an hour of working mostly in silence, we decide to take a break.

"A milkshake sounds pretty awesome right about now," Papi says. "Want to walk over to Jimmy's Diner and grab some mint chocolate chip with double fudge and sprinkles?"

I'm part excited and part nervous. I want to go with Papi, but I also know that Mami would never let me have a milkshake after what the doctor recommended. But it's been so long since I could do this with him, to hang out like we used to, so I decide I should go for it.

"Definitely," I say, following him out of the garage. I hope Mami doesn't text, or worse, video call while I'm drinking my milkshake!

He takes my hand and gives it a gentle squeeze. For the first time since he's returned, I see my dad smile. Really smile.

I smile back because life's pretty good right now. I have a social studies project topic that I picked without Mami's help and Dad trusts me enough to help him fix a broken car. Bonus: mint chocolate chip milkshakes.

# CHAPTER TEN

I'm in such a good mood the next day at school that I decide to ask Clarissa again if Gus can come to her party.

"I mean," she says, out of breath, "doesn't he live really far away? In Park View or something?"

"Yes. Well, just at the edge, but yeah. I'm sure his dad could stick around to pick him up afterward."

"I don't know, Emi Rose," she says. "I'm fixing to invite the whole pep band after my triumphant debut at the pep rally. They all said I did an amazing job."

"You sounded great," I say. "Only one fart sound out of the mellophone."

"You're funny," she says, not laughing. "Anyway, it'll seem strange if he comes when I didn't officially send him an invite, you know?"

The bell rings.

"But I'll think on it," Clarissa says. "That fair?"

"Sure."

"All right, talk to you later."

She starts to leave, then swings back around.

"Hold on a minute. How's your daddy doing?"

"He's okay," I say. "We worked on a car together yesterday."

Clarissa flinches. "Well . . . how nice for you."

We both look around. I try to think of something else to say.

"And we talked," I tell her. "A little, but it was nice."

Clarissa's face sags. "My daddy used to get real quiet whenever he'd come home from a deployment."

I can tell the tears are about to pour out at any moment.

"You okay?" I ask.

"I'm fine," she says. "Sometimes you remember everything all at once, you know?"

"Yeah," I say, but really, I'm wondering if she asks about my dad to have a reason to share things about her own. That's not a bad thing. I just wish she'd be honest.

She turns slowly and leaves for real this time.

I know Clarissa would like Gus if she just gave him

a chance. He doesn't have family in the military, but he's caring and funny and a great listener. I think Clarissa could use someone like that in her life.

After school, Gus and I walk toward Park View to Don Carlos's Grocery Latino. Gus is carrying a huge travel bag along with his regular backpack.

"What's in the bag?" I ask.

"Wardrobe and props," he says, with a mischievous look.

"Oh, Clarissa might invite you to her party," I say.

"That's nice, I guess, but like I said, we'll probably be at the movies."

"What if you convince Barry to go? And Lacey will totally love it if Chinh shows up!"

"I don't want to get their hopes up. Besides, Chinh has a super-strict curfew and Barry and I planned to do some storyboarding, and afterward, I was going to help him with his project."

"Oh, he needs help?"

"Just with animating some of the slides for his presentation," Gus says. "He's a great writer, and he has all this cool knowledge about trees and insects, especially from around here. For his project, he's doing a scavenger hunt of Merryville Woods, where people have to find native trees like beech trees, Southern sugar maple trees, and, my personal favorite, the loblolly pine."

"Why is that your favorite?"

"I like the name loblolly."

"Kind of tickles my tongue when I say it."

"And," Gus continues, "Barry has pictures of strange bugs to look for, like the sphinx moth, the American copper, and the pill bug, which Barry calls the roly poly because it curls up into a little ball when you touch it."

"Wow."

"Yeah, Barry's really smart. But all teachers ever focus on is that he doesn't test well."

Maybe that's something Mrs. Jenkins could help Barry with too. I wonder if she already knows.

"Anyway, tell me how it goes."

"Can't your dad drop you off?"

"Look, I don't think Clarissa wants us there, Emilia. She doesn't exactly hide her dislike."

"I think it's just a misunderstanding. If you two got to know each other better, maybe you could become friends."

"I don't want to ask my dad for that. He likes to get home right after work to be with Daniela."

"I wish I had a sister or brother that my parents could worry about instead of me," I say. "Being an only child, I have my mom and Abuela and even my dad in my business."

"Must be nice," he says. "Having all that attention."

What Gus just said is true, but it stings a little.

Gus kicks a rock along the sidewalk like a soccer ball. It rolls awkwardly off the pavement and into the gutter. He goes to look for it but stops himself before he reaches the drain.

"Hey, remember *It*? Pennywise is one of the best horror creatures ever."

"I couldn't even finish it," I tell him. Who could blame me? *It* is a story about a horrible child-eating clown.

"Pennywise fed on fears. When kids stopped being afraid, he couldn't harm them anymore."

"Still terrifying. I *never* want to see that movie again. *Ever*."

"I'll think about it," Gus says, moving back to the sidewalk. "About Clarissa's party, okay?"

"Awesome. Thanks, Señor Gus."

"De nada, señorita," he replies, only bowing slightly as he continues to walk.

We follow the road to Park View. The path is dotted with garbage.

"I never noticed how dirty it is over here," I say.

Weeds are overgrown. There are a few soda cans and candy wrappers littered about and graffiti sharing messages of *my one true love.*

"It's like the sanitation department gave up after Main Street and just went home for the night," Gus responds.

"Tourists aren't going to come here!"

"Maybe people will decide to clean up after your tourism guide."

The track curves around two parts of town, like it's telling two stories. One with mostly redbrick buildings, little shops, and monthly festivals, and the other a place where messages of love are mixed with garbage.

We're both silent for a bit as we walk deeper into Park View. Two kids play on the swings at a playground surrounded by trees. Someone who might be their grandpa takes turns swinging each kid.

"Hi, Mr. Jackson!" Gus waves.

Mr. Jackson turns around and takes a moment before recognizing Gus.

"Oh, hello there, young man!"

Mr. Jackson waves and quickly gets back to pushing the girl who's swinging toward him at that moment.

"Mr. Jackson takes his granddaughters to the park every afternoon," Gus says. "They live in that house right over there."

Gus gestures like a tour guide while he tells me what he knows of Mr. Jackson's story.

"His wife passed away last year," he continues. "He moved in with his daughter and son-in-law and when they're at work, he watches over his granddaughters."

"He seems happy."

"He is," Gus says. "But his knees aren't so great anymore, and walking his grandkids to Park View Elementary is a trek for him. Everyone thinks it's too far, but he's stubborn."

"Like my abuela."

"Yeah, kind of, I guess. Anyway, it'd be way closer for him to walk his grandkids if they went to Merryville Elementary."

There are a few parked cars on lawns just past the playground.

"It's so cramped here that there're hardly any parking spaces," Gus says. "But we have the best block parties."

"I've been to some of them. They're so much fun."

"Especially the ones Barry's family throws. His dad's barbecue is the tastiest in Merryville. Probably all of

Georgia. And his biscuits, oh my gosh, it's like, that's what God above wants on Sunday after church. Mr. Johnson's homemade biscuits and gravy."

"Wasn't he going to open a restaurant?"

"It fell through. Something about the loan got messed up."

"That's too bad," I say, admiring the tall oval-shaped trees lining the street.

"Barry says that's the Southern sugar maple, a smaller cousin of the bigger, more famous maples out by Canada and the Northeast."

"Ours may be smaller, but they're mighty," I say. In the autumn, these trees look like the sun has kissed them and turned their leaves into flames.

"You know," Gus says, changing the subject. "Sometimes I think Clarissa is nicer to you because she thinks you're like her."

"She just has trouble making new friends. She likes things to stay the same."

"Yeah, maybe. Is that why she's talking smack about the redistricting?"

"I've only heard her mention it once. But I've been kind of focused on my dad lately."

"Well, it's not just her. I heard some kids at school

talking about how bad it's going to be if Park View kids come to Merryville next year."

"What's so bad about it?"

"I don't think they care about Park View. I mean, look at how much our sanitation department cares," Gus says, motioning to the ground. "The district doesn't stop to think that it might be worse for the Park View kids."

"How so?"

"It's like when I moved from Alabama. I didn't know anybody and I had to get used to the way the school worked. Now imagine if, on top of that, nobody wanted me there. That's what it's going to feel like for any kid from Park View if they have to get transferred."

I've gone to Merryville schools my whole life. I don't know what I would've done if I had to suddenly move to a completely new school. I probably wouldn't like it at all.

"Anyway, since your project will take people to Park View, maybe it could bring some attention to the neighborhood. Get people to talk about it."

"Maybe. I like your project because it will be so fun," I tell him while crossing the street.

"It will be fun to shoot, but I hope it shocks people too," he says.

"It's going to be great," I say.

"So is yours," he tells me. "It's different. Off the beaten path, as they say. Not like Chinh. He's doing his on the sporting venues in town, starting with the football field."

"Why?"

"Because he wants to try out for football next year and he's sucking up to Mr. Richt."

We both laugh.

"Grocery store up ahead," Gus says. "But first—"

Gus pulls out his camera and starts filming. "I think we can shoot part of the movie here. It can be like the start of *El laberinto del fauno*."

Gus became obsessed with Guillermo del Toro after seeing *Pan's Labyrinth*. It's not really a movie for kids, but Gus's tita let him buy it because he only showed her the English cover and she thought it was about Peter Pan. It is *not* about finding Neverland. There are monsters and a really scary creature that has eyes on his hands.

We watched it on Gus's iPad in Abuela's office one day last summer, tucked in next to the shelves of oil and hanging car fresheners for sale. Gus got a headphone splitter so we could listen at the same time. The movie terrified me, and Gus tried to make me feel better by telling me the story behind it.

"It's an allegory for the Spanish Civil War," he said.

"That pale man with the eyes on his hands is so creepy!" I told him.

"Guillermo del Toro created him to show how he feeds on the helpless and doesn't want to share his riches," Gus said. "This is what I want to do with my life, Emilia."

"You want to feed on the helpless?"

"No, silly," he said, laughing. "I want to make movies."

After some test shoots, we reach the edge of town where there's a strip mall.

"¡Por fin llegamos!" The store's sign comes into view— the large blue D in DON and the even bigger C in CARLOS'S followed by LATINO GROCERY STORE in cursive white letters underneath.

The lot has a few cars and trucks parked with several people strolling in and out. Waiting for us on the other side of the lot are the automatic sliding doors.

The first thing we see when we walk through them is the familiar display of meat with various types of sausages and steaks lined up neatly. The signs identifying each meat are in Spanish first and English second. Chorizo is the only one that just says chorizo. I guess that delicious, slightly spicy sausage doesn't need a translation. You either know what it is, or you don't.

Don Felix is there and greets us both.

"¡Hola, chicos!"

"Hi, Don Felix," we say at the same time.

"¿Todo bien? ¿Tus padres, eh, tu abuela, Emilia?"

"Sí, Don Felix."

"Muy bien, muy bien." He throws a piece of beef on the counter.

"Dile a tu abuelita que tengo lomo de Argentina," he says, smiling.

"Okay, Don Felix," I reply. "I'll be sure to tell her."

Don Felix nods and hums to himself while expertly slicing meat.

"What's up with the massive grin?" Gus asks.

"I think Don Felix has a crush on my abuela. And I think, by the way Abuela acts around Don Felix, she might feel the same."

"A little romance in the twilight of their lives, huh?" Gus says. "Que cute."

There are various piñatas dangling from the ceiling alongside colorful papel picado.

"Do you think people actually buy those piñatas?" Gus asks.

"Why would they hang them up there? Somebody must buy them."

I've never been here without Abuela hurrying me down the aisles, so I make a point of taking my time to look around. There is a whole wall of Goya products. You can buy beans in cans or beans in bags—red, black, brown, and some white ones with a little black dot in the middle. With so many colors, why does Abuela only buy the black beans? They're not my favorite.

On a shelf, I spot a whole bunch of dried peppers in bins lined up in several rows.

"Tita makes birria with those ancho and guajillo peppers," Gus says. He points to the black chile and dark red pepper next to it.

"Oh my gosh, the beef in her stew falls apart in your mouth. And with her warm corn tortillas to dip in the spicy broth. That's probably my second-favorite dish in the world next to lechón asado," I tell him. "Mr. Johnson's barbecue is right up there also."

"For sure," Gus says. "Hey, do you remember the time I wanted to help Tita, but I didn't use gloves to handle the peppers and I burned the side of my eye?"

"That's right! You were screaming until Tita wiped

your eye with a paper towel soaked in milk."

"It's the reason I'll never step foot in the kitchen again."

"Come on, Gus, it's not that bad! And besides, you know how to take care of it now."

"My eye caught fire, Emilia. The pain was excruciating."

"I like that word."

"It's a good one. And one that's appropriate when rogue guajillo pepper essence attacks your eye socket."

Gus points to a bag of pink candy that says DULCES DIANA NOUGAT FRESA.

"I love strawberry candy!"

Mom and Abuela would *never* let me eat this. I pick up the bag and inspect it.

"It's from El Salvador," I tell Gus, who has moved down the aisle.

He squeals suddenly, and I know he's found his favorite candy. This is the aisle where they keep the good stuff.

"Look!" Gus picks up a tube with a lime-green label and a wild-eyed character on it. "Who's scarier: Pennywise or the creature on the Pelon Pelonazo label?"

"I don't know," I say. "But it won't stop me from eating that tangy tamarind perfection."

I rush over and take a bag of Pelon Pelonazo. I feel so

tempted to buy both candies! But I already broke the rules with Papi, and I should probably just stay away.

I head toward the register to see Don Carlos.

"Emilia, mi querida. ¿Cómo estás?"

"Hola, Don Carlos," I say.

"Gustavito, ¿qué tal, hijo?"

"Bien, gracias, Don Carlos."

We catch up for a bit. I tell him about my school project and that I'm adding Don Carlos's Grocery Latino as the first stop on my tour.

"Pero, mi querida, ¡qué honor! ¡Gracias!"

He seems pretty flattered and says that I can ask him anything.

I use my phone to record him. He gives me some information about how the store runs and how he orders the foods he stocks on shelves. He explains how many employees he had when he started and how many he has now. It's a lot if you include the Mexican restaurant in the back. He says he opened his store in 1996.

"¿Por qué?"

Don Carlos says that when he moved here from Venezuela in the mid-nineties, there was a huge demand for food products from all over Latin America and the Caribbean.

"Why?"

"Había mucho trabajo en esos tiempos," he says.

"There was a lot of work here? For what?"

"¡Pues, para las olimpiadas en Atlanta!"

"Atlanta hosted the Olympics?"

"Claro."

I love the summer Olympics! I *love* the Pan American Games, where countries from Latin America compete in summer sports, *and* the US games, even some of the European ones that lead to the Olympics every four years. The swim meets and track and field and gymnastics. How did I miss that the Olympics were in Georgia? Like, forty minutes from my house, Don Carlos says!

This store is practically the Pan American Games of food supply. Don Carlos has labeled the aisles with flags from different countries.

"You have so many different types of food, Don Carlos. From everywhere!"

"Somebody can be far from their country, but if they have food from home, they feel less far away."

"Yeah," I say, holding the nougat fresa. "Thank you, Don Carlos."

"De nada, corazón," he says. He takes out his iPad and flips it around to take a selfie.

"Para los fans del mercado." He catches me and Gus in an awkward pose.

"The grocery store has fans?" Gus asks.

"Bueno," he starts, "we have over ten thousand fans. Cool, ¿verdad?"

It is cool.

"And to be interviewed by a local reporter is going to get so many likes. There, I posted."

Don Carlos takes another picture of the carnicería display.

"One more picture so the fans know the meats we have on sale."

"Two posts in a matter of seconds," Gus says.

"That's twice as many as I post a day!"

"Seriously."

"Oh, Don Carlos?" I say.

"¿Sí?"

"Before I forget, I'd like to buy the Diana nougat fresa, por favor."

I hand him a few dollars and put the candy in my back-pack. Gus eyes me.

"Living on the edge there, señorita."

"It's not for me," I tell him.

"Yeah, right," he teases. "It's for your 'friend' who really wants candy because she can't eat it when her mom is in town."

"You shush!" I shove him gently, but he pretends to fly back and almost smacks right into a pillar. "You're ridiculous, Gus Sánchez."

I decide to visit Don Felix at the meat counter one more time.

"Don Felix," I ask him. "¿Cuándo llegó a Merryville?"

Don Felix thinks for a moment.

"Yo vine en el noventa y quatro," he says.

"1994! You've lived here that long?"

"Sí. Trabajé en construción en Atlanta. Ayudando con el estadio."

"The stadium? You worked on that?"

"Sí."

"How did you become a butcher in a grocery store?"

"Pues, hay que trabajar," he says, handing me a small package. "Pa'que tu abuelita lo prueba."

I take the wrapped-up meat—a gift for Abuela—while Gus wiggles his eyebrows.

"QUE. CUTE."

"You, stop!" I thank Don Felix. He nods and offers a shy smile. Walking through Park View, looking around Don Carlos's grocery store, and talking to people I've known forever makes me realize I haven't been paying attention as much as I thought. I make a mental note to talk to Don Felix and Don Carlos more often. Even when I don't have a project to do. You don't know what you might miss if you don't bother to ask a question.

Gus senses it's time to leave. "¿Vamos?" he asks. "To film?"

I hate to disappoint Gus, but I feel like poking around more for my project. "I think I need to go back to the library, Gus. I'm sorry. Can we film tomorrow?"

"Um, sure," he says. "I'll just film more scenery today instead."

I feel bad because Gus brought his bag and everything, so I think about a compromise.

"I'll go to the library real quick and then we can meet up at the shop. I need to check in with Abuela first, but after we can film before it gets dark. Cool?"

"You sure? It's okay if we go tomorrow."

"Yeah," I say. "I just want to look at news from the year Don Carlos started his business. So I'll have more to say in my tourism guide."

"Sounds like a plan, Señorita Torres."

"Gracias, good sir," I say, starting our handshake.

We both head out of the store and walk in the direction of the library. We pass the playground and watch Mr. Jackson slowly chase after his granddaughters as they laugh and run away from him.

I check my phone and find a few missed texts. One is from my dad saying he's gotten some other good ideas from the book I left him. I respond with a smiley face and he replies with a thumbs-up and a heart emoji. The other is from my mom about doing homework together. I tell her that I'm already working on something on my own. She sends me a heart emoji and tells me she'll talk to me later. Then she sends two more texts about how proud she is of me and how much she misses me. Mom gets supertexty when she's not around.

I walk into the library with a mission to find out more about the 1996 Olympics in Atlanta—the year Don Carlos opened his store. I'm not sure if that information will be necessary for my project, but I think a good tour guide should know their history.

Mrs. Liz tells me to go right ahead and start digging.

"And the microfilm machine is fixed! Changed the fuse myself."

"Cool, Mrs. Liz. And thank you."

I rotate the articles using the little knob on the right. The first one is about Centennial Olympic Park. I know that place. It's in Downtown Atlanta. There's a cool fountain in the shape of the Olympic rings that kids can splash in. It's right next to the Georgia Aquarium, and across from one of my favorite places, World of Coca-Cola!

I learn some things about Centennial Park that I didn't know, like that it's twenty-one acres. In order to raise money to build it, people could make donations by buying bricks that were laid as pavers for the park. For thirty-five dollars, people could write special messages engraved on the bricks. The article says the committee raised over seventeen million dollars.

I do the math in my head. That's almost five hundred thousand bricks, which is a lot of bricks to lay! I examine the black-and-white picture and read that there were tan and dark red bricks lined up together in groups throughout the entire structure. The flags around the park represented all the countries that participated in the games. It's like Don Carlos's store aisles, only with way more countries.

The next article about the Olympics is a recap of the opening ceremonies. It describes the impressive "pyro-technics show," which I think just means fireworks and stuff like that. And something Papi would probably like: there was a fleet of Chevys on monster-truck wheels that drove around the Olympic track.

There's another article about Gloria Estefan singing a song called "Reach" at the closing ceremonies. Abuela loves Gloria Estefan! She calls her Gloria, like she knows her, but I'm pretty sure they've never met. It's probably because they were both born in Cuba and came to the United States around the same time.

I keep scrolling and come across an article about a woman named Sara J. González who was hired by the Olympic committee to do Latino community outreach in Atlanta. She was a small-business owner and Cuban immi-grant who fought for immigrant and minority rights in Atlanta. There's even a park named after her. It's the first park named for a Latina in the state of Georgia. I wonder if Abuela knows about her.

I take another reel and slide the film into the machine. Each time, I read a little faster.

My doctor told me that I show signs of what she calls "flow." It's like seeing a faraway planet I *really* like and thrusting the *Millennium Falcon* into hyperdrive to get there. Basically, when I hone in on something I'm interested in, it's hard to distract me from it. I'm 110 percent in the flow right now.

The next article I read is about how Mexicans were recruited to Georgia in the mid-nineties to help finish construction for the Olympics. According to the article, immigration enforcement was suspended during this time to encourage workers to come to Georgia.

I think about the almost five hundred thousand bricks. Then I think of Don Felix. He must have been one of the workers who came to help finish the job before the Olympics started. The article goes on to talk about the "boom" in immigration and how much of it can be traced back to this moment.

I load another reel, which is dated pretty recently. Before I switch it out for an older one, something catches my eye. It's a story about immigration laws in Georgia, but it's about what's happening with them *now*. The laws are stricter and give local law enforcement the power to check the immigration status of people who can't provide identification when they're asked. The article talks about a man who was deported to Honduras because he didn't have immigration papers, even though he's spent most of his life in Arizona and his kids were born there!

Abuela and Mami were both born in Cuba. What would happen if someone forced them to go back? What would happen to Papi? Where would I end up?

None of this seems fair. Who makes the rules about who gets to stay somewhere and who has to leave? My mind is a million stars blinking at once. I think about the Arizona man and his kids. Who's going to take them to school?

Mr. Jackson walks his grandkids to Park View Elementary every day, but his girls might have to move to Merryville. Even the decision of which school you go to isn't yours.

I chew the tip of my pen and *tap-tap-tap* it several times on the table. My face feels hot.

"You okay, Emilia?" Mrs. Liz comes out from stacking books to check on me.

"I'd like to print this out, Mrs. Liz," I tell her, already looking for the print button.

"Sure thing, hun."

I use tabloid-sized paper, the biggest the library has, to get as much of the article as possible. I thank Mrs. Liz and grab my things.

"You bet," she says.

My Merryville tourism guide suddenly has more questions than answers.

# CHAPTER ELEVEN

Back at the shop, I immediately look for my dad. He's not there. I'm disappointed, because I need to talk about what I just read. I text Mom while standing next to a blue Chevy Impala. Actually, it's not blue. It's *blue velvet metallic*. Gus's dad told me once that vehicle paint isn't just blue or red or yellow.

"Tienen nombres interesantes," he said.

"¿Por qué?" I asked him.

"Pues ¡para darles *más vida!*" He waved his hands in the air expressively as he shouted, "More life!" Gus didn't seem interested in any of this, but I was. His dad showed me the VIN on the lower part of the windshield by the driver's side.

"Este es el número de identificación de este vehículo."

"Vehicle identification number?"

"Eso," he said. He told me that every car has a special number indicating all the details about the car.

"Cada carro es especial," he said, smiling proudly.

I think part of him would love to paint cool designs on cars. He keeps a sketchbook that I've seen him draw in while sitting on one of the oil drums next to his stall. He makes really cool designs between bites of Tita's special torta ahogada, a sandwich stuffed with cuts of seasoned pork and soaked in tomato sauce inside a crispy baguette called birote. It's exactly as delicious as it sounds.

I get a text from Mom.

Mom: Hey! How's it going, mi amor???

Me: i found some articles for my social studies project . . .

Mom: Cool! Tell me about them!

Me: i didn't know that atlanta hosted the olympics

Mom: Yeah! But isn't the tourism guide about our town?

Me: yeah. but when i interviewed don carlos, i found out some stuff and i read about a law that made me upset. can u talk?

Before I can text anything else, Mom is already video calling.

"Hey!"

"Hey, Mom."

"What's making you upset, boo?"

"This law! Can police really kick people out of the country if they don't have an ID?"

I tell her about the Olympics and the workers who were encouraged to help when the laws were not enforced. My mom is quiet for a bit while she thinks of what to say.

"Okay," Mom starts. She takes a deep breath. "Let's break it down. You know I'll always be honest with you, right, mi amor?"

I nod because I know it's true.

"Instead of giving these workers a path to citizenship, the government just expected them to do the work and leave. Then some people got upset when the workers didn't leave, even though they have contributed greatly to our state economy and have made a home here."

I can feel a lump in my throat. I think Mami sees it. "But that's why we vote—so we can have people in office who help create the type of place we want to live in. Whenever you see injustice, mi amor, you have to speak up and fight back. It's everybody's responsibility as humans."

Of all the blinking stars in my head fighting for my

attention right now, I see a small one flittering around like a firefly. Glowing then turning dark. Glowing then dark. I want to follow it to see where it goes. But how do I chase something that lights up and then disappears into the darkness? How do I keep it lit so I can see where it leads me?

"Injustice has long, winding roots, mi amor. Did you know that in the sixteenth century, over one million African slaves were brought to Cuba?" Mom asks, bringing me back to our conversation.

"Really?"

"Yeah. And those people, in bondage, brought traditions that helped shape Cuba's cultural identity."

"You're talking about the Yoruba, aren't you?"

"Yes, they came from Western Africa, to be exact. Much of what is Nigeria today. And those traditions and histories that have made their way to Cuba and other parts of Latin America are undeniable and they continue today. No matter how many people try to erase it or deny it."

Mom tells me that injustice didn't start today, and we must learn from history. I think about what I've learned doing this project.

Mami breathes in slowly. "You keep digging, mi amor.

I have a feeling your tourism guide is going to bust some heads."

My mom laughs. Her mouth is wide and her eyes are squinting with joy.

"Proud of you, boo. And remember that I'm here if you want to talk about what you find."

"Thanks, Mom."

"K, gotta go. Let's talk tonight."

"K, love you."

When I end the call, the Chevy is staring at me from its stall like a motionless metal animal waiting to be cared for.

It's just another car with a different set of problems. Sometimes people try to fix their own cars, but they don't know how and end up causing more damage.

"Prognosis, Doctor?"

"Oh, hey, Gus!" I didn't see him walk up behind me. "Well, the car is going to need a new rim and we should check the alignment," I tell him.

Gus is flabbergasted. I like that word. It was on our language arts vocabulary exam a few weeks ago. I studied a lot for that test because Ms. McKennen said if the whole class passed, she would give us a Friday fun day, which is basically freewriting. I don't really like writing, but the rest of the class does, and I didn't want to be the one who messed it up for everyone. So I studied and when the grades came back, Ms. McKennen said she was "flabbergasted" by our performance.

"How on earth are you so good at this?" Gus asks.

"I don't know," I tell him. "When I'm interested in something, I don't usually miss details."

"If you keep helping your dad, you're going to run this shop one day."

Gus's comment makes me smile, and I think about the thumbs-up emoji Papi sent me.

"Wanna go over to the woods now?"

"Yep. Let me just tell Abuela." I wonder whether I should talk to Gus about what I found at the library.

There's a man at Abuela's office door. As we get closer, I recognize him—it's Mr. Renter. Jay from my homeroom is his grandson. We wait behind him as he struggles with the door. He pulls and pulls until Abuela walks over and pulls the door open from the inside.

"Thanks, Aurelia," he says. "I always forget: it's push from the outside and pull from the inside."

"No problem, Bill. How are the grandkids?"

"Fine," he says, standing about a foot taller than Abuela.

He's wearing his Renters' Lumber collared shirt tucked neatly into his jeans. He keeps his sunglasses on as he talks to Abuela.

"My grandson wants to try out for eighth-grade football next year, but I just don't think that boy has it in him, you know?"

"He'll put on some weight and grow over the summer," Abuela says. "Boys grow between fourteen and sixteen. And his grandfather is tall, eh?"

Mr. Renter puts his hand lightly on Abuela's shoulder.

"Yeah, that's true," he says, turning to me and walking over.

"How you doing there, Emi Rose?"

"Fine, thank you, Mr. Renter," I say.

"School going well?"

"Yes."

Mr. Renter turns to Abuela and pays his tune-up bill. He walks over to his truck, pops the hood, and inspects the work.

Mr. Renter has been coming to Abuela's shop for years, but he always struck me as someone who would prefer to get his oil changes somewhere else if we weren't so conveniently located by his lumber business. I remember one time he kept exaggerating his English to Agustín and making a point to show him where the carburetor was on his truck. Agustín knows more about car engine parts than even my dad. He knew exactly where it was.

"Hey, you mind washing my window here, son?" Mr. Renter stares at Gus, who turns back to see if anyone is behind him. "I'm talking to you."

"Uhh, I don't work here, sir."

Mr. Renter's eyebrows arch and he shakes his head.

"Well, thanks again, Aurelia," he says. "You all should come by the house for dinner. Would love to see Toni now that he's back from duty. We'd like to thank him for his service. And besides, Cindy is cooking up some sweet potato casserole!"

"Sounds delicious, but maybe another time, Bill," Abuela says. "I'm going to take this young lady shopping for dresses."

"Okay," Mr. Renter replies. "You have fun shopping with your nana, Emi Rose."

"Thank you," I say. My first thought is: sometimes I want to tell people that's not really my name. It's Emilia Rosa. And my second thought is: *what?* Once Mr. Renter leaves, I ask Abuela why I need a dress.

"You don't want your LEGOs anymore," she says. "And you're asking to go to parties. You're becoming a señorita."

"Abuela," I start, "I am *not* becoming a señorita. You're getting the wrong idea."

"Nonsense. Your quinceañera will be here before we know it."

"What? Abuela, that's, like, three years away!"

"It's never too early to start thinking about these things."

I shake my head in frustration.

"And you should start thinking about wearing perfume, too. Como una mujercita."

The sound of a duffel bag landing on the floor startles me. Gus seems completely mortified. Why would Abuela think it's okay to talk about this in front of Gus? He's my best friend, but there are some things you just don't say out loud.

"Abuela! You are so embarrassing!"

I grab Gus's duffel bag from the floor and ask him to follow me.

"Gus and I are helping each other with our social studies projects," I say abruptly. "We're going to the woods to do some filming."

"Today?" Abuela says. "Weren't you just at the library?"

151

"Yes," I say. "But we have more things to do. Like film-ing extra scenes. Right, Gus?"

"Huh? Oh! Yes!"

Abuela eyes us suspiciously, like she's trying to decide what to do with this information. Before she says anything, I lead Gus out of the office.

"Be back in one hour!" she shouts.

I pick up the pace to get as far away from Abuela's "mujercita" talk as possible.

We enter the woods through a different part of town this time. The light of the afternoon reflects off the tree branches and bounces off the rocks and patches of earth all around the woods.

"Nature gives the best light." Gus marvels as he cap-tures the scene with his camera.

We find an old gazebo that was crushed by a tree. It must have fallen during one of the hurricanes that swept through a few years ago.

Gus explores the old gazebo. "Who do you think this belonged to?"

"Not sure," I say. "Maybe it's from an old estate aban-doned years ago?"

"I think another story is brewing—a star-crossed-lovers kind of tale where one love waited by the gazebo but the other never showed up and she became so sad that she cried herself to death."

"Sad," I say.

"And her name is Llorona."

"Isn't that already a tale? La Llorona?"

"Sí, pero that's from Mexico and we're in the woods of Georgia, so I have creative license."

"Fair enough."

I slide my hand across a beam and catch a giant splinter in my forearm.

"Ow! Darn it!"

Gus rushes over and almost immediately runs the other way. "Jesucristo! Tita tells me not to use the Lord's name in vain, but that looks so painful!"

"Ouch! Hang on." I drop my backpack and focus on my forearm.

"Emilia, we should go back. That could get super-infected. If you don't . . . ¡Aye, Díos mío! Emilia!"

I pinch the splinter with my pointer finger and thumb and rip the giant sucker out of my arm. Gus almost faints.

"You okay?" I ask.

"Sí," he says. "But I would've gone to the hospital."

"Not for a splinter, silly!"

It doesn't hurt that bad anymore.

"¡Por favor! Let's change the subject before I puke," Gus says.

The rustle of our feet against the leaves sends a quiet echo through the woods. The farther we walk into this new trail, the more it feels like we've left Merryville for a different world. The forest comes alive with the possibilities of the stories all around us. The thought of anything bad happening in or outside these beautiful surroundings seems impossible.

"See these roses here?" Gus points to a shrub with small flowers with white petals and a yellow center. The whole shrub is in full bloom.

"Isn't that our state flower?" I had to memorize all the state symbols for a geography test last year. Mom made me repeat them over and over and over again until I saw the state nickname (Peach State), state song ("Georgia on My Mind"), state vegetable (Vidalia onion), state fruit (peach), state dog (adoptable dog), state bird (brown thrasher), and even the state prepared food (grits) all swirling in my head for days. "It's the Cherokee rose," I tell him.

"Yeah," Gus says. He turns his camera to the shrub. "I read about the Cherokee rose online."

"What's the story behind it?"

"It's about the Trail of Tears of 1838," Gus says, pointing to the flower, "and what was taken from the Cherokee Nation. These seven leaves here are for the seven Cherokee clans. The center is for the gold stolen from them. But it wasn't just gold that the white people wanted, it was land, and soon after, they forced the Cherokee clans to leave their homes. The Cherokee had to endure the harsh journey to Indian Territory out west. And in the middle of winter! Without enough food, or medicine, or anything."

"How awful!"

"Yo sé," Gus says. "Y también, I read that thousands of lives were lost, including many children. So each rose that grew along the trail represented a Cherokee mother's tears."

"A flower so beautiful also tells the story of such a violent past," I say, thinking about my conversation with Mom earlier about the Yoruba.

"Yeah," Gus says, still looking at the Cherokee rose.

We're both quiet for a minute, just observing.

Not too far from the shrub is a beech tree trunk. It

looks like the muscular, veiny calf of a giant. Leaves are just starting to grow back on its branches after the winter made them bare. They reach up toward the sky, all twisted and tangled, nearly blocking out the sun. Trying to figure out which branch belongs to which tree is like a gigantic puzzle.

"I think I came up with a title for my movie," Gus says.

"Before you even start filming?"

"I'm going to call it *The Merryville River Monster*."

"Seems a little obvious," I say.

"It's a working title."

He starts to explain his idea for the story. It's a mix of the water legend from Gus's library book and something he invented. In it, a young woman gets lost on her way home and ends up deep in the woods. She stumbles upon a river where she encounters the creature on the other side of it. The creature watches but doesn't move. Then it disappears.

"Mr. Richt said to find places to share with visitors," Gus says. "To me, Merryville is made up of a bunch of stories. Plus, he didn't say we couldn't get creative."

"Very true," I tell him.

"Now, let's talk casting," he says. "How would you feel about playing the girl *and* the creature?"

"Wait," I say. "Both? Why don't you ask Chinh or Barry to help?"

"I thought a choice like one actor playing both roles could say: what if we are the very monsters we are afraid of?"

"That's deep, Gus," I tell him.

"Es la verdad."

Gus sets down his duffel bag and unzips it. He pulls out an old tarp, a piece of aluminum, and a Baggie filled with lugs and washers. Gus grabs a few branches and places them on the laid-out tarp. Next he takes nails and a hammer from the duffel bag and secures the pieces of wood to the tarp.

"Um, Gus?"

"Darn thing!" he says, ripping the nylon.

"Gus?" I repeat.

"What's up?"

I get closer and ask him for the hammer. He hands it to me and I use the claw to take the nail out of the tarp. I grab a small and sturdy piece of wood and place it beneath the tarp, then take the wood Gus was trying to hammer down and put it on the other side. I hold the nail steady while I hammer both pieces of wood together. When I'm done, the wood is holding steady against the tarp.

"She's an actor *and* a carpenter!" Gus says.

"Definitely *not* an actor. And I don't really know carpentry," I tell him. "I'm just good at figuring out puzzles."

I take the other pieces of wood and start to assemble the Creature. Gus uses a twig to take out a few dirty rags from his duffel bag to add to the costume.

"Are those from the auto shop?" I ask, taking one of them.

"I got them out of the garbage," he says. "You shouldn't touch those! Your hands are going to smell forever."

I sniff my hands and realize Gus is right—the odor of oil and grease is heavy. There's something comforting about it, though.

Gus sets up his camera and I put on the monster costume that's really just a tarp with some dirty washcloths and tree branches stuck to it.

"It's like I'm a pile of garbage that's come to life," I tell him.

"Don't worry. It's really cool on video," Gus says, looking through the camera.

After we film a few scenes of me as the creature wandering around the woods, Gus pulls out my costume change.

"Okay, that was amazing, Emilia! Now you're going to play the cop not listening to the kid describe the terrible creature she saw in the woods."

"I'm the cop, too?" I ask. "Where's the kid?"

"The camera," he says. "Talk to the camera like it's the kid."

"Um, okay?"

We film the cop scene a whole bunch of times because I keep doing what Gus calls "breaking character," which means I keep stopping to ask Gus what a cop is doing in the woods if the monster is supposed to be a mystery.

"I'm filming nonlinearly," he says. "It's out of sequence with the narrative, but I'll put it in order during edits."

"Oh," I say, not really sure what he's talking about.

I finally get the scene right, and we move to the next one, where I play the role of "concerned citizen."

Before we know it, it's almost six thirty, and I tell Gus we should get going.

"Yeah," he says. "Hey, thank you for helping me, Emilia."

"De nada, director extraordinaire."

We pack up Gus's things and make our way out of the woods while Gus talks about Guillermo del Toro.

"His movies have layers. That's the genius of his work. He's trying to say: lo que es diferente isn't what we should fear; those who are unchanging are most terrifying."

"Gus, you're dropping a lot of wisdom today."

The tracks ahead remind me of how trains connect different parts of Georgia to Merryville. Like Atlanta. What happens in one part of the state affects another. I can see Gus wondering what I'm thinking about, but I don't have the right words to explain all the thoughts bouncing around in my head.

A previous mayor called Atlanta an "international city," but I see it with a whole lot of contradictions. How does the city of Merryville, with its different neighborhoods and schools, fit into all of this? I don't know as much as I thought about my own home, and it's getting the *Millennium Falcon* in my brain ready for another jump into hyperdrive.

# CHAPTER TWELVE

When I get home, my dad is on the sofa, watching TV. He doesn't hear me come in. The house is quiet because Abuela isn't home yet. Usually there's a pan sizzling in the kitchen or the rumble of the dryer in the laundry closet, or the creak of wood under our feet. I check my phone and see Mom sent me a text a little while ago. We keep missing each other.

I walk over to my dad, but he still doesn't turn around. I wonder why he wasn't at the garage earlier. Maybe he didn't feel well and needed to come home. I want to do something to cheer him up, like bring him flowers.

Papi makes a noise and moves his head from side to side like he's in an argument with himself. He's sleeping, but it doesn't look like he's resting. I go outside and pick bright pink azaleas from Abuela's flowerpot on the front porch. I rush over to the sofa and throw my arms around his shoulders, flowers and all.

"Hi, Papi!"

He jumps up, totally startled. His body seems tense and his face looks angry.

"Geez, Emilia! Don't spring up on me like that!"

His hands are balled up into fists and he's staring at me all wild-eyed.

I stop and remember what Mom said.

There are a few rules we have when Dad is home.

We never play dead.

We never shout.

We never make sudden noises or drop things on the floor on purpose.

We never, ever, sneak up on Papi.

I step back and wait for my dad to feel calm. I remember what happened the time the "Welcome Home" balloon popped one year. That's why Mami doesn't do a big celebration anymore. She was there that day to comfort him. I think about what she did.

She stood in front of him but gave him enough space to move around if he wanted to. She waited a little, then asked in a gentle voice if he needed anything. Next she put her hand in his until he made eye contact.

In this moment, Papi holds a sofa cushion.

"Papi," I say, slowly approaching. "I'm sorry."

He doesn't respond.

"Papi?" I say again, this time reaching the sofa and placing my hand on top of his.

We lock eyes for a minute.

"You okay?" I ask.

He nods. "I'm sorry I scared you, Emilia," he says. His body deflates a little and his arms sag at his sides.

"I'm sorry I sprung up on you," I tell him. "I forgot."

My dad stares at the flowers on the floor.

"These for me?"

I nod.

He picks them up and holds them to his nose.

"You know, I took that papier-mâché flowerpot you made me a few years ago everywhere I went," he says. "You remember that?"

"Yes," I say softly. I made it for him in my fourth-grade art class. I cut out tulips, roses, and daisies using colorful construction paper and arranged them in the pot.

"I carried one of the flowers in my rucksack during every daily patrol. They brought me luck on those four-hour treks."

I hadn't asked him about the papier-mâché pot or the construction-paper flowers because I figured he'd lost them, or they'd gotten ruined. That's why last year I decided to start sending video files. To give him something that wouldn't break. Does he remember those, too?

"These look like the ones Abuela has outside," he says.

I'm embarrassed. Just as I'm about to apologize again, Abuela walks in through the back door.

"¿Qué pasó?" is the first thing she says. How does she know something happened? She wasn't even here!

"Nada, Mami," my dad says. "Emilia gave me some flowers."

Abuela takes the flowers and steps closer to inspect my face.

"¿Y esa mugre?" Abuela asks, wiping dirt from my cheeks. "You said you were going to go study for your project."

"I was," I tell her. "Gus's project is about monster myths from Merryville. We went to the woods to film."

"Your face is covered in dirt, Emilia," Abuela says. Then

she notices my sleeves. "And your clothes are filthy. Is this the way a young lady is supposed to look?"

My dad steps around the sofa. Just as I hope he's going to come to my defense, he moves past me toward the stairs.

"This seems like a discussion for the ladies of the house. I'm going to go upstairs."

I shake my head and feel my cheeks get hot. Why doesn't he ever take my side?

"Don't look at me with that face, Emilia Rosa," Abuela says. "You are running around in the woods with Gustavo Sánchez, playing monsters, when you should be concentrating on your studies and spending your time in more appropriate ways for your age."

"Fine, Abuela," I say. It's harder than usual to control my frustration.

"When you leave this house, you represent this family. What are people going to think about us?"

I want to yell that all she cares about are other people. But then I remember the Yoruba rule Mami taught me: "We must respect our elders." Why are there so many different rules I have to follow?

Before I can say anything, my feet take over and I rush up the stairs. I close the door behind me and throw myself on my bed, bury my face into my pillow, and scream as loudly as I can. I scream until my voice cracks and my temples hurt. I wish I were back in the woods, playing in Gus's imagination.

I must have fallen asleep, because the next thing I remember, I'm groggy and my phone is buzzing. I hope and pray that it's Mom, but it's just an alert from one of my puzzle games. I decide to try her anyway.

Me: love you mami

The squiggly lines pop up and I get excited. Maybe she has a moment to talk.

Mom: Hi, baby! You good? You wanna talk more about your project?

The truth is, I don't want to talk about my social studies project or my math homework or anything like that. I just want to hear her voice.

Mom: Hey, how's it going with Dad? He's not talking much.

I think about how to respond. My mom and dad are really close—like best friends. They joke around with each other. Snuggle on the sofa and hold hands. They both love comedy specials, and when they're home, they go on dates to eat chili dogs at Jimmy's Diner and sometimes drive all the way to Atlanta to watch a Hawks game when it's basketball season. When they're both home, it's like they breathe easier. Even Abuela doesn't challenge them as much when they're together.

Mom: You okay, mi amor?

I don't want to say the truth, because that would feel like telling on Papi. I could tell her about Abuela trying to buy me dresses and saying I have to act like a lady. But that would probably only cause an argument. And sharing any of this with Mom won't bring her home. So I just type:

Me: good. miss u. bye.

Before my phone lands on my bed, Mom calls.

"Hey, Mom." I throw myself onto my bed and stare at the ceiling.

"Boo, I know you're going through a lot right now. I've been lighting candles to bring good spirits home to you."

"Thanks," I say, sitting up to see myself in the mirror. My wavy red hair is big, and freckles dot my entire face. "But, Mami, I don't think that's going to work. I don't have Yoruba in me."

"Why would you think that?" she asks. "Did Abuela say something?"

"No," I tell her, lying back down.

"Baby, you are *my* daughter. When you came into this world, you got parts of me whether you believe it or not."

"It doesn't look like it. I don't very feel Cuban sometimes."

"When I get home, we're going to talk more about this, boo. But for now, what I can say is that there isn't one way to be Cuban. There isn't a 'good' way or a 'bad' way. And yes, some people will make you feel like there is a good way or a bad way based on how you look. But that says more about them than about you. It's my promise to you that I'll always tell you about where you come from and your history. The more you know, the stronger you will feel."

"I'm super-flustered, Mami. All these things I've found in my research. I'm tired and angry and worried at the same time."

"I don't blame you."

"Like, could that happen to me? Could I be deported because my mother and grandmother came from another country?"

"No, mi amor. The law currently protects those who were born in this country."

"What about you or Abuela?"

"We're both citizens now."

"What about Don Felix?"

"From what Abuela tells me, he moved to Atlanta from Mexico in the nineties, then Alabama to work at the chicken plants, then Merryville, where he got a job as Don Carlos's butcher."

"Can he be forced to leave?"

Mom doesn't say anything for a moment.

"I hope not, but honestly I'm not so sure, mi amor. As I understand it, he's tried to apply for citizenship for years, but it's a long and involved process. They don't make it easy and sometimes it seems like the same rules don't work for everyone."

"It just doesn't seem fair."

Again, Mom is quiet.

"No, it's not fair," she finally offers. I can hear her exhale. "I'm sorry it's been such a whirlwind, baby. Maybe I should change my flight and come home sooner—"

"No!" I yell, stopping her before she can finish. "It's fine, Mom. Don't worry."

"How can I not worry?"

"It'll be okay."

"Talk to Papi," she tells me. "He's a little down right now, but he's an incredible listener and supporter."

It doesn't seem like it, but I don't tell Mom that.

"Okay, I'll text you tomorrow."

We finally hang up. It feels like I'll always be chasing that firefly in the dark.

Mom sends me an emoji that explodes into a million hearts across my screen. I put my phone down and decide to grab my backpack to distract myself from how I feel. I pull out a few folders and take out some crumpled papers from the main zipper compartment. There's a form Mr. Richt gave the class this morning. I didn't bother reading it because I was rushing to get to language arts.

I straighten out the edges and read. They want us to confirm our address in Merryville and the grade I'm supposed to be going into next year. My parents have to sign and return it to the administration by next Friday.

I toss the wrinkled page onto my desk. Mami isn't here to sign it, and I don't really want to ask Dad to do anything right now. Papi still feels like he's thousands of miles away.

I start my proposal for Mr. Richt's class. I list my tour stops: Don Carlos's Grocery Latino and the library. Two stops is probably not enough, so I think about other places to add. Maybe the Cherokee rose shrubs in the woods? I think tourists would like to see the beautiful roses and learn about their history. I write that down. Three places seems like a good start for a tour around town.

Next I write a few sentences about why I chose these locations. Finally I propose what I want to investigate. I slide the paper into my social studies folder and put away my backpack. It's almost seven thirty.

Papi's preferred dinnertime has come and gone, but that doesn't stop Abuela from trying to get us out of the house for "un poco de aire." She opens the door to my room and walks right in. She never bothers to knock or ask if she can enter. Abuela just assumes she can.

"Let's find a place to eat out," she says. "It's still not too late, and I think we all need some fresh air."

I don't disagree.

"Can we finally go to Delucci's?"

Dad pops his head into my room.

"The garlic rolls are awesome," he says.

"The best," I tell him.

"Mind if I come in?" he asks.

I nod and stand up.

"Hey, Sweet E," he says.

I was five when he came up with that nickname. "Something that only *I* get to call you," he said.

"You haven't called me that in a while, Papi."

"True," he says. "Are you too old for it?"

"I don't mind," I say.

Abuela stands between us and ushers my dad out of the room.

"Cámbiate primero," she says to him. "And wash your face."


We arrive at Delucci's and the hostess seats us at a booth near the window. She hands us three menus and we set about looking at the various choices, when my phone pings. Abuela shoots me a look as I check the screen. Gus has sent me an image of the *Pan's Labyrinth* movie poster, only he's photoshopped the image to read:


**LOS MONSTRUOS DE BOSQUE MERRYVILLE**

**WRITTEN AND DIRECTED BY**

**GUSTAVO MIGUEL SÁNCHEZ**

**STARRING**

**EMILIA ROSA TORRES**


I have to admit that I like the way my name appears on a movie poster. Gus changes film titles a lot. I start to tell him that, but I hear a *tap-tap-tap* on the table. Abuela is watching me intently.

"You shouldn't be on your phone at the table, Emilia."

"Sorry," I say.

I put my phone in my pocket. It's noisy in the restaurant. People are talking at all the tables, and the booths lined up against the walls are full. The lighting is soft at Delucci's, and there are red-and-white tablecloths on all the tables. The clanking plates and silverware are just enough to make it a little distracting. I've gotten used to it for the most part, though. Mom said to look at one object if I get uncomfortable, and focus on it.

A few guys from town approach our table and say hi to my dad.

"Great to see you out and about, Toni!"

"You been here a few days and we haven't seen you around, buddy! Let's hang out soon!"

My dad mostly just nods and doesn't offer much in the way of small talk. His eyes dart around the room. I follow his gaze as the restaurant sounds get louder.

Doors opening and closing. A person asking for the soup of the day. A lightbulb above one of the tables goes out and the people sitting under it try twisting it. My dad's knees bounce up and down, up and down, while he fidgets his thumbs. He flashes an uneasy smile at Abuela, but Abuela seems oblivious to what's going on. I get it. I know exactly what Dad is going through.

"Papi," I say, trying to get his attention. "Papi?" I try again, but he's clearly distracted. Watching him look around is making me nervous. The noises start to crowd my head. Abuela is talking about something, but I'm not listening to a word. It's all too much.

"What can I get you!" a server says suddenly.

My dad and I both jump back.

"Dang, man!" Papi says. "Is it necessary for you to yell like that?"

The server seems scared. My dad is very muscular, and when he's upset can be kind of intimidating.

"I'm sorry, sir. Are y'all ready to order?"

Papi points to the shrimp Alfredo and asks for a Coke. Abuela chooses the lemon-roasted chicken with vegetables and a small Caesar salad with the dressing and croutons on the side. She repeats the "on the side" part.

"I'll have the angel hair pasta Bolognese with an extra serving of garlic rolls."

"Anything to drink?"

"Water is fine, thanks."

We wait for our food when I suddenly hear a loud bell followed by a group of servers clapping and cheering. The commotion across the restaurant is a bunch of servers gathered around a table singing the most obnoxious rendition of "Happy Birthday" in the world. I love Delucci's. I hate when someone celebrates a birthday here.

My dad puts his napkin on the table and gets up.

"I'm going to get some air."

He leaves through the dining room, around the hostess stand, and through the doors to the sidewalk. My dad paces a bit, and I can see through the window that he's finally calming down. His noise has dimmed, but mine continues bouncing around in my brain like a pinball.

Even though I know this isn't my fault, I still feel guilty.

The server arrives with our order, and Abuela hands back the food.

"We'll take this all to go," she says.

The waiter seems annoyed that we just made him go through all the trouble of setting us up for dinner only to box our food.

"You serious?" he says. He's young, like maybe he's still in high school or something. And he's skinny like

PVC pipe. He's all limbs and seems uncomfortable in his oversized red-and-black Delucci's button-down shirt.

He walks back to the kitchen with the plates. I overhear a couple talking and turn around to see that they have a little girl who's about six or seven in the booth with them.

"Yo creo que va a ser bueno."

"Sí, Pedro, pero ¿qué vamos a hacer con la transportacíon? ¿Y todos los niños aquí que no hablan español?"

"Pues, que aprendan. Isabel aprendió hablar íngles."

They're talking about schools—the redistricting. It sounds like they might have to move their daughter to Merryville from Park View for first grade.

The server returns with our to-go boxes and a large brown bag. He drops the check and moves to the couple I've been listening to behind us.

He interrupts their conversation to take their order. "Um, I'm sorry, but I don't speak Spanish," he starts. "Are you going to order?"

The two parents look stunned. Their daughter blows bubbles in her plastic water cup with a straw.

"Well, sir, you interrupted our private conversation," the woman says. The server seems confused. "Now that you're here, I'd like to order the spaghetti Bolognese."

I snort as the waiter scribbles down the order in his notepad. Even Abuela finds it hard to hold in her chuckling.

As we get up to leave, Abuela winks at the couple with their daughter.

"Buenas noches, señores. Que disfruten de su cena."

The little girl waves goodbye to us. On our way out the door, Abuela flags down the manager.

"That young man should learn a little Spanish," she says. "And to be more polite as a server."

A small bell dings as we head outside with our boxed-up food to meet Papi. I'm a little surprised Abuela said anything to the manager. She's usually much more reserved in public. Dad taps his feet impatiently like he's ready to go. Abuela seems disappointed. I know how she feels. Nothing we do for my dad seems to be working.

# CHAPTER THIRTEEN

Clarissa hasn't been on the bus for a few days, so I haven't seen her as much. She says her mom has decided to drive her since things might change a lot if the school board votes to redraw district lines and allow Park View kids to come to Merryville Middle.

Before Mr. Richt's class starts today, she reminds me to fill out my address form and have Papi sign it.

"We have to show them that there are already enough students at this school," she says. "We don't need any more."

I wish Clarissa heard the couple last night at the restaurant. I don't think she's actually talked to anyone from Park View.

"So, what's your tourism guide on?" she asks. "Mine's on the Red, White, and Boom Boom Fourth of July Festival."

Even though we're only supposed to have our places

picked out at this point, Clarissa has brought a poster board with pictures of town hall and a few photos from last year's festival.

"You did a lot of work already," I say.

"Did you know we have one of the oldest Fourth of July celebrations in northern Georgia?"

"I didn't."

"What's yours on?"

Before I can tell her, Jay Renter barrels into class.

"Hey, everyone! Check out *my* awesome project!" He's holding a magazine article about the one state football championship Merryville High School won in its history, way back in 1971. "I printed out the schedule of the football season so tourists can check out every game!"

"Who's going to want to check out a middle-school football game, Jay?" Barry asks from his desk.

"My grandpa will!"

Barry just shakes his head and organizes his folder. Clarissa's face looks like she ate a sour lemon. She leaves our corner to talk to Lacey about her project, and Gus takes his seat in front of me.

"You and Mr. Nguyen can't both do a project on the football team," Mr. Richt says.

"But, Mr. Richt!" Chinh pleads. "Jay is doing it on the football *season*, where *I* am doing it on the actual football stadium. Mine is an architectural ode to the gridiron!"

"Intriguing. I'll allow it if you two partner up."

Chinh and Jay stare at each other like the other one farted.

"I'll change mine," Chinh says.

"Wait, you don't want to do a project with me?"

"Well, no."

"That's not cool, man."

"Jay, we had to work on a project at the beginning of the year and I did *all* the work."

"But you're so smart!"

"Forget it. I'll do a guide to local agriculture. Or migrating birds. Anything but working with you again."

"All right," Mr. Richt says, reading off class names. One by one, my classmates share the places they're putting in their tourism guide.

Lacey's guide is about the town's movie house and how it used to be a vaudeville theater in the 1920s. She says there can be daily tours of the old theater that end with a movie or show of some kind.

Gus shares his movie poster with the class, and I'm

not sure everyone gets it. They probably haven't seen *Pan's Labyrinth*.

"Miss Torres?" Mr. Richt says. "You're up."

My walk to the front of the class feels like hours. When I get there, my hands start shaking. I can see why public speaking freaks out Mom. I was going to ask her for tips, but I wasn't sure if she'd text back in time. So I'm doing this on my own.

"Miss Torres?"

Mr. Richt signals for me to continue.

"Sorry," I say. I study my notes and take a deep breath.

"Umm . . . I've lived here all my life, and what I think most people would like to visit in Merryville is, umm . . ."

Gus gives me a thumbs-up.

"My family likes to cook, and a lot of my memories have to do with food. I spend a lot of time with my grandma shopping for ingredients, so I thought I could take visitors to the place where we buy ingredients to make the food that makes us feel good."

"Wait," Jay says. "Are you saying you're taking visitors to Kroger? I wouldn't go on that tour."

A few kids laugh, but they stop when Mr. Richt tells them quit it.

"Kroger doesn't sell specialty items to make Cuban food; only Don Carlos's Grocery Latino does and—"

"That's not even in Merryville," Clarissa interrupts while raising her hand.

"Um, it's in Park View, and Park View is in the same city, just a different neighborhood."

I see a few confused faces in the crowd, but I keep going. I know they'll be interested in the next part.

"Okay, so I asked Don Carlos when he opened his store, and he said 1996 because there was demand for it. I wanted to know why there was so much demand in 1996. Did you know that's the year Atlanta hosted the Olympics?"

I get excited all over again and I start talking about some of the other information I found.

"Do you know how Atlanta built Olympic Village so fast? Immigrants. The government made it easy for immigrants to help. But guess what! After it was built they expected people to leave, but they didn't. And there are laws trying to get rid of people even though the government basically invited them, and I'm wondering, Mr. Richt, why we aren't learning about this in school because Georgia is all connected and what's happening in other places affects Merryville. Oh, and I want to take tourists to the library because that's where I learned all of this. They can get a library card and learn more for themselves. And finally, they should visit the Cherokee rose shrubs all over the Merryville woods because they're pretty but they also tell us about the history of the Trail of Tears, which we *really* need to learn in school also!"

I take a huge gulp of air because I think I forgot to breathe during my presentation. Everything came out— even stuff I didn't write down. I turn toward Mr. Richt, a little embarrassed, but he nods like he's impressed.

"Wait," Clarissa blurts out. "I mean, I love you and all, Emi Rose, but most of what you said has nothing to do with touring places in Merryville."

"Actually," Mr. Richt says, "this is what I was hoping all of you would do: dig in. Ask big questions. Look into places that are personal and also have depth. Don't be content with turning off your brains after class. For us to be tour guides, we have to analyze the information that's around us. Tour guides are historians in some ways."

Part of me feels proud, but the other part really wishes Mr. Richt hadn't said that about my project. Now everyone is going to think I was sucking up to him for a good grade.

"Miss Torres even went so far as to connect history with present-day policies," Mr. Richt adds.

"I don't get it," Jay says.

"Great work, Ms. Torres," Mr. Richt says, ignoring Jay completely. "I look forward to seeing what you come up with."

A lump sets in my throat as Mr. Richt walks back to his desk.

When class is over, Clarissa follows me into the hall.

"Sorry I jumped in like that, Emi Rose," she says. "I still think your project is more about Park View than Merryville, but I guess Mr. Richt didn't want you to start all over, huh?"

"I guess," I tell her, but I know that's not what he said at all.

Clarissa has strong opinions. Last year, on a field trip to the Georgia Aquarium, Clarissa moved all the way up to the front of the school bus, right behind Mrs. Loretta, and kept giving her directions on how to get there. With her phone in hand, Clarissa would tell Mrs. Loretta to "exit here" and "turn right in three hundred feet."

You could hear Clarissa's GPS app barking driving directions in a British accent while Clarissa repeated them. Mrs. Loretta mostly ignored her. I did see her roll her eyes once or twice in the rearview. Our science teacher finally told Clarissa to turn off her phone and let Mrs. Loretta drive.

"Hello? Earth to Emi Rose?"

"Hmm?"

Clarissa stares at me with a sideways look.

"Sorry, what did you say?"

She takes my hand and walks with me down the hall.

"Emi Rose, you've been one of my best friends since kindergarten. I don't think you need to go 'uncover' things for some school project, you know? I mean, you're Emi Rose! You've always been fun and creative, making cute projects for your daddy while he was away and things like that."

I try to say something, but she talks over me.

"Bless your heart, you got so worked up in there, and I don't want you to get stressed out. It worries me." Clarissa smirks a little. "It's just a school social studies project, Emi Rose. Don't take it so seriously."

I feel like someone just shocked me. Like when you attach jumper cables the wrong way.

"You poor thing," Clarissa says. "Probably overwhelmed with your daddy being home and being all by yourself because your momma left."

"She's on a work trip," I snap. "And my abuela is here."

"Oh my goodness, your granny is the sweetest," Clarissa says. "She's such a good Christian."

I don't even bother telling Clarissa that Abuela's Catholic. What's the point?

"Can't wait for the hang tonight, Emi Rose!" she says. "I confirmed at least twelve seventh graders are going to be there."

"It seems like this 'hang' is turning into a party," I say.

"Shush!" Clarissa says, drawing near. "If I say it's a party, more people are going to want to come."

We pass Gus in the hall.

"Hola, chicas."

Clarissa sighs deeply.

"Hey, Gus," I say.

"I love your project topic, Emilia," he tells me.

"Thanks," I say. "Yours too."

"Well, I've got an amazing actress playing multiple roles, so that's a major reason it's going to be awesome."

My shoulders relax.

"Well . . ." Clarissa butts in. "She's probably not going to have time, Gustavo, so you might want to find another actress."

"Oh, don't worry, Clarissa. You can be in it too if you like."

Clarissa laughs and pretends to wipe tears from her eyes.

"Yeah, right, Gustavo!"

"Well, thanks for letting me know how you *really* feel, Clarissa," he says, then turns to me. "See you after school, Emilia?"

"I'm going to go to the library, but after that, sure."

"Um," Clarissa says. "You have plans later, Emi Rose. Don't forget."

"And Gus is invited, right?"

Clarissa watches Gus then turns back to me. It seems like she might be holding back a scream.

"Why, of course," she says flatly. "Otherwise, what kind of host would I be?"

Gus shakes his head. "Catch you later, Emilia," he says. He turns to Clarissa and bows. "Your Excellency."

My laugh echoes through the halls.

Clarissa smirks. "I just love how he doesn't care what other people think."

# CHAPTER FOURTEEN

After school, I go to the library and see Mrs. Liz sitting behind the reference desk.

"What brings you in today?" she asks.

I tell Mrs. Liz about my presentation. She says the connections I'm making—from the jobs created because of the Olympics to the resulting immigration patterns to new policies—are fascinating.

"Does that mean you want to look at the recent news and politics sections of some local newspapers? Maybe some opinion pieces, too?"

"That's probably a good start," I say. "Do you think my visitors are going to be bored if I add too much stuff?"

"Well, it's your tour," she says. "What would *you* want them to know about your town?"

"If they start the tour at Don Carlos's, I'd like them to know why he is here in the first place. And maybe get them to think about how his store helps the community."

"I think that's wonderful. I'm sure plenty of tourists would want to know that."

"Can I use the microfilm machine?"

"Of course!"

It takes me a while to find my first useful article. I glance outside a few times to make sure it isn't nighttime yet. I've been sitting for a long time, so I get up and stretch. Mami would probably be proud of my research.

Mrs. Liz comes over to see what I'm up to.

"Having a good stretch, Emilia?"

"Mrs. Liz, do you know how many Latinos live in Georgia?"

"I can't say that I do, Emilia," she says. "But I can do a quick search for that information, if you'd like."

"I can't use the Internet," I remind her.

"Sweetie, I'm a librarian. My one job is to make sure my patrons have access to the information they need to educate themselves."

"This is why Merryville Library is a stop on my tour!"

Mrs. Liz winks and starts typing. Her fingers move quickly across her keyboard.

"According to the most recent available data from the

Pew Research Center, there are over nine hundred thousand Latinos living in the state of Georgia."

Nine hundred thousand people. Some who were born here in Georgia, some in other parts of the United States, some in other countries. Students, shoppers at Don Carlos's Grocery Latino, business owners, horror filmmakers.

Just then, my phone buzzes with a text from Dad.

Dad: Come meet me at the garage!

He doesn't offer any details, so I figure I should go straight to the shop to see what's happening. It's getting late anyway.

"Hey, Mrs. Liz, I have to go. But thanks again for all your help."

"I'm at your service, Emilia," she says. "Nothing makes me happier than feeding an inquisitive mind!"

I'm not sure what she means. I start to go, but I think of one more question to ask.

"Mrs. Liz, do you know where else I can find information about unfair laws? Where should I look?"

She takes a moment to think about it.

"Well, I can help you find resources if you stop by tomorrow," she says. "Also, since you can't use the Internet, maybe a parent or guardian can check out the American

Civil Liberties Union website for you? That has a ton of information," she says.

I type that into my phone and wave at Mrs. Liz as I head out.

The sky is clear on my walk home, and I can feel the first signs of humidity in the air. It can get pretty cool in Merryville. It even snowed one year when I was younger. It wasn't a big snowfall like they have in the Northeast. More like flurries. Papi was outside with me and together we raised our hands to the sky, mouths open wide so the snowflakes could land on our tongues.

Abuela and Mami were on the porch. Mom was wrapped in her big fluffy sweatshirt and Abuela wore earmuffs and ski gloves that she'd bought when she saw the forecast. She kept telling us that we were going to get pneumonia. Whenever the temperature drops, Abuela insists I wear the warmest clothes to avoid getting sick.

I'm excited to see my dad at the shop. I hope he's feeling good today. I have a lot I want to tell him.

When I get there, Papi says he has a surprise for me.

"I ordered it over the weekend and it's at home. But I

have to work on this hood first. It's almost done.

"Can I watch?"

"You're wearing closed-toe shoes, so that's good. Now, let's see if we have some safety gear that fits you."

I follow him to the tools and gloves and welding helmets. I try to put on a pair of coveralls hanging on a hook by the shed, but I look like I was stuffed into a potato sack with two drawstrings.

"That's not going to work," Papi says, lifting the coveralls up so my head disappears inside the suit, which smells like an old gym bag.

Next, Papi hands me a helmet. "Actually, hang on."

He rushes over to Abuela's office while I wait, and he comes back with a helmet that looks like it belongs to an X-wing pilot. I try it on and it drops forward, and suddenly my head is surrounded by a sweaty sock smell. It's like nobody has cleaned the inside of this helmet. Ever.

I flip the shade down and everything goes dark. I can only make out tiny fractions of light from the outside. When a shadow approaches, I lift the shade. Papi hands me a fresh bandanna.

"Don't put that stinky thing on without your own bandanna. Plus, it'll give you a little more support."

"I need a whole other head to fit into this, Papi," I say, taking off the helmet and placing it back on the table.

Papi digs for some protective goggles and hands them to me. "Use these and stay back here while I work."

"Why can't I be close to you?"

"The weld arc can literally make you blind. It's like looking at the sun. And you don't have any protective clothing that fits. Actually"—he takes off his long-sleeved flannel shirt and puts it on me—"better put this on as well. Just in case."

"Papi," I say, my arms disappearing inside the long sleeves. "I'm like a hundred feet away from where you're going to work. This seems like overkill."

"Just wear it, Sweet E. I always made sure my unit was safe above all else."

I grumble but agree to use the goggles and watch from a distance.

He clamps the hood on top of the workbench outside. Before he slides down the shade on his helmet, he looks back and winks. Papi takes the welding gun and, with a flick of his finger, it lights up. The *crack-crack-crack* echoes across the shop as he bonds metal to metal, and I try not to look at the sparks.

He welds a few tacks on the hood then stops.

"So, what I'm doing here," he says loudly while pointing to two small pieces of metal, "is making as straight a bead as I can, connecting these."

"Like it said in the book?" I yell back.

"Yeah, but this isn't a book," he says. "You have to be careful. The welding gun is incredibly hot."

As my dad gets back to work, I feel a rush of excitement. I want to use that welder so badly! Papi flips up his shade and inspects his weld. I look back at the helmet I tried on before. There's a strap inside. I can tighten it so it fits better.

While my dad's busy, I pick up the helmet and pull the straps tighter. I take the bandanna and tie it around my head and keep my safety goggles on. The helmet is still pretty big, but it fits better. I dig around the box for gloves. When I find the smallest pair I can, I carefully make my way to my dad.

He stops working immediately.

"You're not following the rules, Sweet E," he says. "I asked you to stay over there."

"I put on all the gear, like you, so I thought maybe I could try to weld something. Maybe?"

He shakes his head, but can't help but grin.

"Nothing stops you when you set your mind to something, huh?"

"Nope," I say, trying to make him smile.

"All right," he says, checking my helmet to make sure it's secure enough. "One highly supervised weld. Okay? No more."

"Yes, sir!"

Papi clamps down the curved metal onto the workbench then hands me the welding gun. I get used to how it feels while my dad steadies my hand.

"It can burn you. Be careful, okay?"

I nod in excitement.

Papi says a bead is when the tip of the welding gun melts the metal, creating a line that connects pieces to one another. He lets go of my hand and steps back. The gloves I have on are big and hard to move with, but I try to keep steady. I can feel the intense heat waiting to be released.

"Aim, then flip the shade down when you're ready," Dad says, pointing to the helmet.

I do as Papi says, and I can barely see through the dark glass. My breathing echoes inside the helmet, but it doesn't fog. I feel secure even though the helmet is still too big. I pull the trigger on the welding gun as it touches the metal.

The heat rises and pours out of the gun, sending sparks in every direction. The dark glass protecting my eyes lights up, and the *clack-clack-clack* illuminates sparks all around me like stars dancing on a moonless night. They die down as I release the trigger. I place the welding gun safely on the workbench and flip up my shade.

Papi is beaming.

"How'd that feel?"

"Awesome," I say.

He comes over to look at my bead line.

"Not bad for a first try. Not bad at all. I can't wait to show you your present!" he says excitedly. "You'll be my partner working on this car."

Partners. My dad and I are going to be partners. Just like before.

I feel a surge of energy and calm at the same time. He tells me to step back now so he can continue working.

"Until you get gear that fits, okay?"

I nod, a little disappointed. But he doesn't send me all the way back to the shed. He lets me stay a little bit closer.

"Don't take off the goggles. At any point."

"I understand, Papi."

He moves on to welding the side panels next to the hood. He explains what he's about to do before he starts.

"We're going to make inch stitches along here," he says then turns back, aims, and pulls his helmet down.

Every time he finishes a weld, he pauses to talk.

"My days are so different now, you know?"

I nod even though I don't know.

"A normal day out there started pretty early," he says, almost like he's talking to himself. I hardly even breathe. "I'd swing by the chow hall as soon as the sun was up, for scrambled eggs with cheese and ham."

He stares out for a moment, like he's thinking about what to say next.

"Our eggs were probably local or something, because that's the thing we never ran out of."

"You like eggs, Papi, so that's good."

"Yeah. Anyway, next it was off to the shower trailer for a quick rinse. We had it pumped out of the local river and into tanks on base. It was pretty gross. Poo and all kinds of other stuff floating in it sometimes."

He starts to laugh a little. I guess that means it's okay for me to laugh too, so I do.

"Man, that stuff was nasty! Had to make sure it didn't get in my eyes or mouth."

The thought of my dad having to sometimes rinse in poo water suddenly makes me feel horrible. "I'm sorry, Papi."

"Wasn't all bad," he offers. "Just some rough parts at times. Met some really good people over there. Not just in my unit. And I loved my unit."

I want him to keep talking. Maybe he'll say something about my videos.

"So how's the social studies project going? Mom told me about it. Seems like a cool idea."

I tell him about my research.

"You're just like Mom, Emilia. Neither one of you gives up until you come to the truth of something."

He nods like what he just said makes him happy.

"All right, so I made an inch stitch here, no weld, inch stitch here, no weld. You see?"

"Yeah," I say, walking closer to inspect. The helmet doesn't feel so big anymore, and I've gotten used to the stinky sock smell inside. We both stare at the Shelby.

"Clarissa seems kind of mad at me," I say. "Like she doesn't want to hear anything bad about Merryville."

"Clarissa's reaction doesn't surprise me," he says. "I think some people prefer to stick their heads in the sand."

"What do you mean?" I ask him.

He points at the frame rail and tells me he's going to make three quick tacks where he cut out a seam in order to bond two small pieces of the rail in place. "Well, if you find out your neighbor's life isn't perfect and you're unwilling to help them, it forces you to examine who you are. Some people don't want to do that."

For once, it seems like my papi understands what I'm saying and is taking my side.

"Hey, I think we need a new nickname for you after today, Sweet E."

"What's that?"

"Chispita," he says. "Little spark."

"I like it," I tell him.

Papi turns off the welder and we put all our safety gear back in the shed.

"Hey, it's right around dinnertime. You hungry?"

"A little."

As we clean up, I think about how easy it is to talk to

my dad tonight. Maybe he's finally relaxing. Maybe he's ready to talk about everything.

"Hey, Papi?" I feel a fluttering fire in my stomach, nervous but sure at the same time.

"Yeah, Chispita?"

"I'm just wondering," I say, my voice steady but my chest all thunder and lightning. "You know those videos I sent you? Can you tell me why you never talked about them or sent one back?"

My dad shifts his weight. He seems uncomfortable. He gets up and walks over to the shed. I hear a few grunts and then he starts mumbling.

"We're having a really nice night here working together," he says just out of earshot. "Now is not the time."

I get off my stool and look at him, but he doesn't say anything else. He's watching me from the corner of the back lot like a wounded animal afraid of a hunter who's just popped out of a bush.

I start to wonder if Papi is one of those people who likes to keep their head in the sand.

# CHAPTER FIFTEEN

I get home exhausted. I tell Papi that I'm not hungry, and go up to my room to think about something I have more control over, like my social studies project. At least it's information that isn't going to run away when I ask questions.

Mr. Richt said we couldn't use the Internet, but I'm alone, so I decide to connect. I pick up my phone and look at the note I made when I was at the library. My computer takes a few seconds to power up, and I search for the American Civil Liberties Union of Georgia. At the top left of the page it says *ACLU Georgia* and under it the words, "Defending Our Rights to Equality, Liberty, and Justice."

I read through several articles and cases. One says that the Board of Elections proposed to close voting locations in an area where mostly African American people live. One of the locations is right near Park View!

Another post is in Spanish, with hard-to-read legal information.

I click to a new section. There is a quote from James Madison, one of the Founding Fathers and the fourth president of the United States:

> *"America was indebted to immigration for her settlement and prosperity. That part of America which had encouraged them most had advanced most rapidly in population, agriculture and the arts."*

Mom says we have to vote to change laws we don't like. But what if laws make it hard to vote?

It's like I'm flying in circles, looking for somewhere to land. I remember the woman I read about, Sara J. González. She didn't sit by and do nothing. She fought for immigration rights in Atlanta. I know I have to do something, but I don't know what or if a kid can even make a difference.

I type in "Merryville and Park View Schools" to see if anything comes up on Google. The county public school website has a photo of the school board on the home page. Under the Agenda tab, there's an entry for the next public hearing on the proposal for redistricting elementary through high school students.

It seems like there will be several public meetings before the vote. One to introduce the redistricting, which already happened. The second to hear public opinion, which happens next Thursday. And the third, which will take place in front of the community in a month, is for the vote.

I open up a new tab to look for more articles. There's a map of the school district. The whole district is diamond-shaped, with Merryville right smack in the middle and Park View on the outside looking in. Park View is a neighborhood of Merryville, yet the map shows it as being separate.

At the bottom of the page, in the comments section, parents and other community members are worried about overcrowding. Some say it's more about "safety" when students don't share similar "values." My head is like one of those centrifuges where astronauts train that I saw in a movie. Around and around and around it goes until . . .

Abuela enters my room, like always, without knocking.

"I set up a fund-raiser for church this Sunday," she says. "I asked your father to come help you."

"Help me? With what?"

"With the toy sale you volunteered for. At the church."

"Abuela," I say, confused. "I didn't volunteer for a toy sale."

"For the LEGOs and toys you wanted to get rid of? I thought we could sell them and donate the money to the church."

"Okay," I say, because honestly, I like that idea. "Abuela, have you had something happen to you because you're an immigrant?"

By the stern look on her face, I can tell she doesn't want to talk about this.

"Did you know that people are upset about the school redistricting proposal because they think kids from Park View are going to be a 'bad influence' on the kids in Merryville?"

"No me gusta que estás leyendo esas cosas." She doesn't approve of what I'm reading. "Eso no es un proyecto para una niña de doce años. The adults will take care of it."

I don't understand. Abuela thinks I'm old enough to start planning for my quinceañera, which is not for another three years, but I *shouldn't* be learning about something that affects my town and my family right now?

Abuela changes the subject before I can say anything.

She asks me if I want to go dress shopping with her tomorrow.

I exhale loudly.

"Mira," she says. "Your father can come with us. Maybe we can grab some dinner in Cartersville. You know, have a nice evening together. What do you think?"

I remember our "nice evening" at Delucci's. And the last time I went shopping with Abuela at Plaza Fiesta near Atlanta, it took me twenty minutes to figure out how to get into a dress that had so many layers and puffy parts, I could hardly fit my arms through. The slip was really itchy and felt more like sandpaper than silk. The dress came with a thin belt that I had to wrap around twice to get it to stay in place. It pressed down on my stomach so hard that I worried I'd accidentally pee on myself. I waddled out of the dressing room, afraid to put my arms down because it was surely going to cause itching in other parts of my body.

"¡Qué linda!" Abuela said, examining me.

"I can't move, Abuela," I replied. "And it feels like a thousand mosquito bites in the summer. I have to take this off."

Mom was with us and couldn't stop laughing. It wasn't funny.

Abuela leaves, defeated, and my dad knocks on the door

shortly after, while I email myself the websites I found. I want to make sure I can access them on my phone.

He steps inside with a box.

"Hey . . . I never showed you the present I got you," he says. He carefully puts a large box at the foot of my bed.

"Thanks," I say.

"Don't you want to open it?" he asks.

I shrug. I don't know how to act around my dad anymore. I can never tell what's going to make him angry.

I peel off the tape to look inside. There's a pair of metallic blue MIG/Stick welding gloves that look just my size. A pair of safety goggles, a really cool shimmering black welding jacket, some black coveralls that look like they're a little big but definitely smaller than the ones at the shop, and an industrial duffel bag. Papi smiles shyly.

"There's more," he says.

I dig further and feel something round secured inside a plastic cover. It's a welding helmet with a fire-breathing dragon painted on both sides. This time, my excitement is impossible to hide.

"Now you can help me in your own gear," he says. "If you still want to."

"I do," I tell him. And I mean it.

His eyes are droopy. His hair is starting to grow out. It seems like he wants to say something, but it's almost like there's a cable around his waist, pulling him back every time he wants to move forward.

"I love it," I tell him.

I admire my helmet. What will be my first welding project? Well, besides rebuilding the Green Hornet with my dad. There's a tree outside my window that almost touches the roof of our house. There was a bird nest there a year ago, but now there are just a few squirrels that run up and down the trunk. Would welding a metal frame into a tree make a safe tree house?

"I think I found two axles for the Green Hornet at an auto shop in Cartersville," my dad says. "I'm going to go pick them up tomorrow and maybe you can come with and later help me weld them together. You can use your new gear."

I nod.

"Cool," he says. "Good night, Chispita."

"Good night," I say.

My dad leaves the room. I put on the jacket, the pair of gloves, and the helmet. I can see *me* lighting up everything I touch. And I can hear the *clack-clack-clack* coming from every direction.

Actually, it's just my phone.

Gus: where r u?
Me: home. why?
Gus: i went to clarissa's. u weren't there

Oh no. I totally forgot about the party! The dragon's scales on my new helmet cast sparkles on my phone.

Me: im sooo sorry gus!!! totally forgot!!!

Gus doesn't answer for a little bit. I can't believe he actually went. I was distracted with my dad and my project and then the helmet, and I just didn't remember. Squiggly lines on my screen let me know Gus is typing.

Gus: its fine. gotta go. my dad just got here
Me: k bye. sorry again

I put the phone down and hope at least Gus had a good time. But by his short responses, I'm worried that he didn't and I feel awful.

# CHAPTER SIXTEEN

Saturday morning starts with my dad moving pots and pans around in the kitchen. He's trying to cook fried eggs but isn't having much luck keeping the yolk from running.

"I can lead a platoon ten thousand feet above sea level, but I can't keep an egg yolk from running," he says. I walk over to the stove and take a spatula to mix the eggs around.

"We can make them scrambled," I tell him. "Do we have cheese?"

My dad pulls out a bag of shredded cheddar from the refrigerator.

"How about this?" he asks.

"And some salsa!" I tell him.

He perks up and dives back into the fridge for the jar of salsa. He opens it and grabs a spoon from the drawer.

"What next, chef?"

"Well, I think some breakfast tacos are in order, no?"

"Oh man, why didn't I think of that?"

I pour the salsa on top of the scrambled eggs and pile on half the bag of cheese.

"Do we have tortillas?"

"Papi," I tell him. "We *always* have tortillas."

"True," he says. "Who taught you how to make breakfast tacos?"

"You remember that time you were home, like, two years ago, I think?"

My dad shakes his head. "Sometimes it blurs into one long deployment," he offers. He stares out the window.

"Well," I say, wanting to keep the conversation going, "Gus's family came over to celebrate you being home. Tita made these incredible corn tortillas and Abuela made scrambled eggs with chorizo and salsa."

"Not sure I remember that, but I'm positive it was delicious." Dad takes a spoon to the pan to scoop some eggs and salsa onto a tortilla. He scarfs it down, but he has to keep opening his mouth to let out steam.

"Man, it's too hot, but it's good!"

We set the table and make more tacos.

"Abuela is at church," Dad says. "She's dropping off your toys for your toy sale before Mass tomorrow."

"I just said I didn't want some of my old toys," I say. "She's the one who came up with that idea."

"She wants to go into Cartersville after that. Maybe we can all go together? I can pick up those parts I need."

"You want to come?" I ask, trying not to sound as excited as I am.

"Yeah, I mean, sure. Let's stop at Shaney's. We haven't been there in a while."

"We haven't been to Shaney's in at least a year," I correct him. It's the best costume and trinket store around.

"You think they still have those cool spears and shields?" he asks.

"I happen to know they do. Gus and I wanted to be knights for Halloween and Mom took us. They have those massive helmets with the horns on the sides. We didn't get them, though, because Mom said they were *way* too expensive for just a Halloween costume. We ended up making our helmets out of tinfoil and cardboard."

"Impressive."

"And they have some new stuff too," I tell him, hoping he really goes with us. It will at least get him out of the house. "Hey, you want to walk through town to get to the auto shop? We can ask Abuela to meet us there once she's done."

My dad slides the dining room drapes over a bit and peeks outside.

"Yeah," I say. "It does look like it's a nice day."

Papi walks with a slight limp. It's not too noticeable, but I can see the way he favors his right leg a little. It's new.

He lets go of my hand and swings his big arm around my shoulders. Together we walk and talk about the weather and about how tall the trees are in Merryville.

Papi must have walked these streets thousands of times as a kid. I've probably done it hundreds of times. Now here we are together, and it feels like we're walking it for the first time.

"Hey," Papi says, interrupting my thoughts.

"Hmm?"

"What are you thinking about?"

"About feet," I say.

My dad laughs a little then takes my hand as we cross the street.

It's cool to think about how people travel in and out of a place. The streets don't change, but the feet walking on them do. I wonder if it's the same with laws when towns change. Do they have to stay the same?

Shaney's is an antique costume store, but what it's known for is its awesome metallic jewelry. A lady named Ms. Marci owns Shaney's. It's named after her daughter.

I hurry over to a section of the store filled with Tolkien memorabilia. There's a replica of Sting, the blade Frodo uses in the Lord of the Rings. Abuela says I can't buy it even though Papi and I play with it. He starts acting like Shelob, the giant spider from the book, while I aim the sword at him to fend him off.

"Van a romper algo," Abuela says, even though I've never broken anything at Shaney's.

"It's fine," Papi says, lunging for an attack. He wraps his arms around me and Sting falls to my side.

"Arrghh!" Papi digs his face into my shoulder and pretends to bite down. I squirm because his face tickles my neck.

"Papi! Your stubble!"

He releases his grip and starts tickling my ribs. I fall and Sting goes crashing to the floor, sending a bell-like sound through the store.

"Every warrior needs a weapon!" Papi says, picking up the sword and handing it to me.

Abuela takes the sword and gives it to Ms. Marci, who places it back in the display case.

"He's right, though," Ms. Marci says, winking. "You never know when a giant spider is going to attack."

My dad moves to another display case. He's like a kid.

"I love this stuff. Always have." He marvels at a double-edged sword. "Isn't this cool?"

"Yeah," I say.

I grab a feathered quill and parchment paper that appears ancient and point it at my dad.

"This is mightier, right, Papi?"

He nods. "Well, mostly, yes," he says, putting the sword back on display. "Where'd you learn that phrase anyway?"

"Ms. McKennen taught it to us. It was an English author named Edward Bulwer-Lytton. He said that in 1839."

My dad shakes his head and laughs a little. "Chispita, you have such a good memory."

"Not for everything," I say, thinking about Clarissa's party.

I take out my phone, hoping to see a message from Gus. I haven't heard from Clarissa, either.

The jewelry section is my next stop, and I find a few cool bracelets and necklaces. Abuela browses the gold-plated ones with saint pendants. I like the metallic necklaces with thick chain mail. I end up buying one with a pendant of a dragon curled around a black ball.

"That's pretty awesome," Papi says.

Abuela buys me a bracelet with a cross and an oval-shaped pendant featuring Saint Teresa.

"Ese dragón no te va protejer," Abuela says, fastening the bracelet around my wrist. She points to her pendant and says, "Esto sí."

"Gracias, Abuela." What else am I supposed to say? I want to tell her that the dragon will protect me too. I really believe that.

On the ride back, Abuela can't stop talking about my quinceañera. My dad mostly doesn't chime in and just drives her truck.

"La quinceañera is what a young woman dreams of her whole childhood."

"Abuela, I'm twelve and a half years old," I tell her, staring out the window. "I've never dreamed about it once. And besides, I don't care if I even have a party."

Abuela flips the visor down on the passenger seat and pops open the little mirror so she can glare at me.

"¿Tienes fiebre?"

"I don't have a fever, Abuela," I say, although the sudden

talk of my quince is warming up my blood vessels.

"How can you *not* care about your quince?" She doesn't even pause for me to answer before she continues, "Everyone will come to celebrate your path to womanhood."

"Abuela, please don't say 'womanhood' again. Can't we just take a trip instead? I'll even go to Cuba if you want."

Abuela is quiet.

"Emilia, tú sabes que mis padres se fueron de Cuba cuando yo era niña."

"I know our family fled, Abuela," I tell her. "But things have changed. The island is different now. People can visit."

"Not me. Not ever. I will die in the United States."

"Abuela, don't be so dramatic. It's not that bad."

I can feel Abuela's anger vibrating off her.

"Mi'ja, there have been tremendous sacrifices made for you to enjoy the life you have in this country. You cannot forget that."

"If that's true, then why do I have to have a quince?" I ask. "They don't do that in 'this country.'"

For the third time in sixty seconds, I've left Abuela speechless. She flips the visor and her face disappears along with any further discussion of my quinceañera.

# CHAPTER SEVENTEEN

I text Mom to let her know what's going on. Nobody else has called or sent a message. I wish Gus would answer my texts or at least call me so we can talk about it.

"Wanna work on the Green Hornet a bit?" Dad asks me.

"Sure."

I take all my new gear, put it into my brand-new duffel bag, and follow him to the back lot at the shop.

"So, since you're such a history buff, wanna learn a little about the 1968 Shelby GT 350?" Papi slowly peels back the blue tarp concealing the car.

"Yeah," I say, feeling a little burst of electricity again.

"Didn't think I was going to have a chance to build it," he says. "But things happen for a reason, right?"

"Yeah," I say, not sure what he's getting at. I place my welding duffel bag down and begin to suit up. After I fix the goggles on my head, I secure the gloves in the pockets of my coveralls and carry the helmet like I'm about to go on a mission to Mars to fix a space station. I don't know if there's actually a space station on Mars but if there was, I would totally look like someone ready to fly up there.

"If I had started it years ago," Papi starts, "I wouldn't get the opportunity to fix it up with you."

I can't stop my lips from curling into a smile.

"I like working on the Green Hornet together, Chispita."

I nod and grin. "So do I, Papi."

He tells me that Carroll Shelby, the designer of the Shelby, made one of the greatest American cars of all time.

"You know that cobra emblem?"

"Yeah," I say.

"It came to him in a dream."

"So cool."

Dad lifts the hood. There's an empty space, and I can see right through to the ground.

"Gotta get the engine parts," he says. "Sand the body, weld the hinge pillars, the axles, get some custom tires. Lots of things to put together."

Papi rubs the inside of the hood with one hand and inspects the grooves in the metal.

"You know the word *resilience* was originally a metallurgical term?" he says, gently dropping the hood closed. "When you bang metal with, say, a hammer, or even melt it with a welder, resilient metal shifts around and bends to absorb the force and the heat."

This is pretty amazing.

"But sometimes metal just gives out when it's put under too much pressure," he says. "Even big strong vehicles like Humvees have a breaking point."

We clear out some space and Papi and I move the welder outside. We run a long extension cord and set up a workbench. Dad brings welper pliers to keep the pieces we're going to weld in place, and then grabs a dead blow hammer to straighten out any uneven metal.

"All right," he says after he suits up. "Can you bring me that panel over there?"

There are a few panels leaning against the frame of the car. They don't look like anything, but I know that every piece matters. Every piece is important to put the whole car back together.

"Where do you want it, Papi?" I ask, lifting the panel over my head.

"Right over here."

We continue to work until Abuela comes out.

"¿Qué hacen?" she asks.

"She's going to help me with the Shelby," Dad replies.

Abuela appears totally confused.

"She doesn't want to work on a car, Toni," she says. "And besides, do you want her getting grease and grime under her fingernails and on her clothes?"

"I want to help, Abuela." I try to sound defiant, but I don't do a good job.

"Aye, mi'ja," Abuela says. "This isn't a LEGO set. Fixing cars is very dangerous."

"I know, Abuela," I say, a little irritated. But before I continue, my dad interrupts.

"Mami," he says. "It's fine. She's a natural."

"She's going to get tetanus from messing around with this machinery."

"She's not going to get tetanus, Mami. And besides, she likes this. Right, Emilia?"

I nod and tell Abuela, again, that I prefer to stay.

"I was going to ask you to prepare dinner with me," she says. "We have to go to the grocery store. You can do more research for your social studies project, eh?"

"I think I have what I need, Abuela."

"Mami," Papi says in a stern voice. "She'll catch up with you later. I want her here with me."

Abuela is silent. Her lips go straight like they did the night Mami told her she was going out west for a conference the same day my dad was returning from deployment. "If she gets hurt . . ." she says.

"She's not going to get hurt," he says. "I'm her dad. I don't ever want her to get hurt."

Abuela is done with the conversation. She storms out to her truck and the engine goes *rev-rev-rev* like an angry growling dog. Then there's the sound of tires kicking up gravel as she backs out of the garage.

"Like I said last time, don't stare at the welding arc," Dad says, turning on the welder and pulling his helmet down to start working. Soon there are metal sparks in its reflection. I look away.

"Listen," he says all of a sudden, lifting his helmet. "I used to really dislike one of my commanding officers. Guy was such a jerk. Never cracked a joke. Never smiled. I didn't like some of the tactical decisions he made either, but I listened. That's a chain of command. And the truth is, he was a good leader. Got the unit safely through each of our patrols. Families can be like that. You don't always like the order, but you've got to trust the commanding officer to do the job."

He refastens his helmet and pulls the trigger on the welding gun again. After finishing a bead weld, he places the gun back on the workbench.

"So Abuela is the commanding officer now?" I say sarcastically.

Dad lifts his helmet to look at me. I can see Abuela in his face.

"I can't be the commanding officer right now," he says. "And your mom is away."

I don't say anything. Instead I just stare at him.

"Listen, you're upset," he says. "I get it. I used to make that same face when I got mad. But don't be disrespectful. She's only looking out for what's best for her unit, you know?"

"Fine," I tell him, not willing to let my frustration with Abuela mess up the really awesome day with my dad.

In between welds, he pauses to talk about being out on patrol. He says that time, he barely knew what month it was. After about an hour the Shelby doesn't look any better. It barely resembles the super-fast classic Mustang it's supposed to be. It's not like working on my LEGOs. I can build a whole model in the same amount of time.

"Next up, we'll get the axles. She'll come back together in no time."

"How long do you think, Papi? Before the Shelby can run again?"

"Not sure, Chispita. But we'll do it," he says. "You and me."

The parts of this old car will take time to find. But we know what we need, at least. We have the puzzle mapped out on paper and the instructions on how to reassemble it. I wish I had a blueprint for my dad. I don't know the pieces Papi's keeping inside. How can I help him put anything back together if he doesn't share the pieces?

After some more time passes, I work up the courage to ask him about my videos again.

"Papi?" My voice wobbles.

"Hmm?" He's focused on the car.

"But why?"

"Why what, Chispita?"

"Why didn't you ever respond to the videos I sent you?"

Papi stops what he's doing and stares at the ground. He exhales loudly and turns to me slowly.

"You know," he says, "I'm trying my best, Emilia."

He lowers his head.

"That's all I can do for you right now."

Papi puts his hammer down and walks off, leaving me with the shell of an old car and a welder that's still on.

The rest of the evening is quiet. Gus still hasn't responded to my texts and I'm worried he's really angry. I even sent Clarissa a text telling her I'm sorry I didn't go to her party. She didn't respond either. Papi has been in his room, watching TV. Mom called him a while ago and they talked for a little bit. I could hear snippets of the conversation from my dad's responses.

> *"Sure. I know. I am trying. No, I don't need to make an appointment. I'm fine. Okay. Yes, I know she is. I know she is. Man, she's got a ridiculous memory! Takes after you, that's for sure. Ha. Yeah. Okay, I'll see you in a few days. Cool, can't wait to hear. I love you. Okay. Love you. Bye."*

I have a memory for things that matter to me. I'm not giving up on my dad, not by a long shot. But he's going to have to talk to me, even if it makes him uncomfortable. Actually, everyone needs to start doing that around here.

# CHAPTER EIGHTEEN

I wake up Sunday morning to my phone pinging like a million times.

Abuela: ¿Dónde estás, mi'ja?

She repeats some variation of "Where are you?" in six different texts and two languages. She's waiting for me at church.

I think about all the times Abuela has forced me to go with her to church even though Mami said I didn't have to. Thanking God for all our blessings is as important as hanging out with friends and playing, according to Abuela. I get that, but the level of involvement she has at church is supernova. She volunteers for food drives, organizes bingo nights. If Abuela is not at the shop, at the grocery store, or at home, she's likely at church, even if it isn't Sunday.

More often than not, Mami would join us, even though she always says she's more spiritual than religious. I guess that means she doesn't need a church to be close to God. That also makes sense to me. Papi has never seemed to care either way, but if he was in town on a Sunday, you better believe he'd go with us. I think we all just wanted to make Abuela happy. Actually, she gave us this really heart-felt speech on her birthday a few years ago about how all she wanted was for her family to accompany her to Mass. She's the master of guilt-tripping.

Abuela texts me a few more times and I tell her that I'm on my way. I finish getting ready and head downstairs, where my dad is finishing his breakfast at the dining table. His phone pings a few times as well, but he just flips it over.

"Good morning, Papi," I tell him, trying to not think about what happened at the garage yesterday. It doesn't seem like that's on his mind either, because he's all cheery.

"Hey, Chispita! Sleep well?"

"Yep," I say. "You?"

"Yeah. Talked to Mom last night. She'll be home in a few days."

"She called me after you two talked."

My phone pings again. Then Papi's.

"Has she always been like this?" I ask, referring to Abuela.

My dad laughs. "She's just hardwired that way. She managed so much after your abuelo passed away that she's just used to being in control."

My abuelo passed when my dad was only thirteen, barely older than I am now. I don't know what I would do without my papi.

"Emilia?"

"Hmm?"

"You okay?" he asks, patting my arm.

I say yes, but inside I'm not okay. I miss him even though he's here, and I'm still mad about what happened at the garage yesterday. I don't mention it because I don't want to start the day upset at each other again.

"Are you coming to church too?"

Papi shifts uncomfortably. "You go," he says. "I'll catch up with you tonight."

"But Abuela's wish."

"I'm not really up for seeing all our neighbors today, you know?" he says. "Tell her next week for sure."

"Okay," I say, not knowing how else to respond. "See you later, I guess."

"Bye, Chispita."

I can't believe he's not coming to church. What if I

didn't want to go? Nobody would let me skip it. It doesn't seem fair.

The parking lot of St. Francis of Assisi is already full. There are a few pines surrounding the property and they always remind me of the way Clarissa and I used to hide behind them to scare each other.

United Methodist across the street has an equally large parking lot, and I can see churchgoers filing in and out. People wave at each other from a distance—everyone is especially nice to each other on Sundays. Clarissa's mom and her grandparents used to take Clarissa to church every Sunday. She would cross the street and we'd play together while our moms chatted or Abuela made small talk with Clarissa's nana. That seems like a long time ago. I don't see Clarissa, but I spot Mr. Renter getting out of his truck.

Past the pine trees, Abuela has set up a long table with all my old toys. A few people browse the bins. It's weird to see people touching my old things.

"I was texting and texting and texting," Abuela says when I approach her.

"I know, Abuela," I reply. "Papi no viene. Lo siento." I don't know why I apologize on Dad's behalf, but I do.

"Ah," she says, surprised. "Bueno, it's just the only thing I ask. It's fine. He'll go next week when we're all back together."

It feels like she has just poured every ounce of guilt she could muster over me, like clumpy oil.

Abuela hands out a flyer to someone standing near the table. The lady hands it back to Abuela.

"Thanks," she says. "But I'll be at the school board meeting on Thursday."

Abuela nods and returns the flyer to her stack. The lady joins another woman. I can hear bits and pieces of their conversation as they pick up and examine my Harry Potter LEGO Quidditch set. I built that thing in six hours.

"Well, imagine," she says. "Our neighborhood is going to be overrun."

"I just don't feel comfortable."

"Me neither!"

Abuela puts little stickers on my old toys and writes prices on them. We sell an assembled TIE fighter for two dollars. The TIE fighter took me about forty-five minutes to put together when I first got it. I was seven. Mami wanted to get me the LEGOs that use power functions, but Dad was home on leave and surprised me with a four-thousand-piece LEGO *Death Star*. Abuela was really annoyed at the expense. When Dad left, Abuela reminded my mom every day how expensive it was, like it was Mom's idea to buy it. Mom mostly ignored her.

"Well, my cousin said those folks from over there have fifteen or more family members living in a house at one time. They've got cars parked on the lawns and it just looks awful," says another woman. She has my Harry Potter Quidditch LEGO set in her hand.

"That's because there isn't a lot of street parking," I blurt out. "And there's only one park for the kids in the neighborhood to play in. Our neighborhood has *three* parks and they're mostly empty."

The two women give me a look like they didn't expect anyone to crack their code.

"I mean, I have *no* problem with those kids at all," one of them says.

"Neither do I!" says the other. They both scoot away from my LEGOs and lower their voices to a whisper. But I have good hearing and I'm laser focused on their conversation.

"You remember that piñata I bought at the Latino store for Eddy's birthday? I mean, I'm completely supportive of that community. But I moved here for the good teachers and the small class sizes, you know? That's all I'm saying."

"Me too," the other replies.

Just then Gus's family pulls up to the church parking lot. Gus steps out of the car and helps get the baby stroller out of the trunk. He comes back around and takes Tita's hand to help her up the church steps. I suddenly feel nervous because we haven't spoken since Friday.

"¡Hola, Tita!" I say, giving her a kiss on the cheek.

"Mi'jita," she says. "¿Todo bien?"

"Sí," I say, looking at Gus. "Gracias."

"Qué bueno." She shuffles over to Abuela next.

Gus's dad and mom move closer, with Gus's dad holding Gus's baby sister, Daniela. Soon the church steps are full. The two ladies who were talking earlier must have felt squished, because they quickly turn around to leave.

"Lo siento, señor." I apologize to Señor Orestes for making him drive to Clarissa's party.

"Yo sé, mi'ja," he says. "Don't worry, okay?"

I spot Gus, but he turns away when we make eye contact.

The church bells ring and Abuela asks me to pack up the table so we can head inside. I think about asking Gus to help me, so we can talk, but he's already guiding Tita to her seat.

"Vamos," Abuela says, putting the rest of the toys inside a cardboard box. She slips the envelope of money we made from these sales into the box and hands it to an usher.

"Gracias, Doña Aurelia," he says. "We can keep the toys for the next service."

I'm hoping Abuela will want to sit in the back pews, but she doesn't. She follows the usher all the way to the front of the church and takes a seat. She pats the wooden bench and makes room for me to sit. It's embarrassing to sit so close to the altar. I have to pay attention the whole time because I'm right in the priest's line of sight the entire Mass.

"I've been meaning to ask you. Did the school send a paper home to sign?"

I think about the crumpled paper jammed in my backpack.

"Yes," I tell her.

"We need to sign it and return it to school Friday," she says.

"How did you know?"

"The school called your mother and asked about it," Abuela says, sounding irritated.

"I talked to Mami last night. She didn't say anything."

"Well, I spoke to her this morning and she reminded me about the paper."

"This morning? It's three hours behind in San Francisco. What time did you call her?"

"Don't change the subject, Emilia. Do you have the paper?"

"Yes," I say, wondering why Mom didn't just ask my dad when she called him. It's like she doesn't trust me to get it signed. I can remember when I want to. I shift on the uncomfortable pew.

"Quédate quieta, niña." Abuela shoots me a look until I'm still again.

"So, what did Mom say?"

"Emilia, Mass is starting. Just give me the form to sign, okay?"

I turn all the way around to see if I spot Gus and his family. Sometimes we'll make funny faces at each other to pass the time. We've almost come up with our own language to communicate silently with our expressions.

Gus is in the middle of the church, on the left side. We make eye contact for a second before he turns his attention to the front of the church. It seems like he's listening, but I can tell he isn't really.

"Presta atención," Abuela whispers loudly.

I tune in to what's happening at the lectern and, in Spanish, the lector says what psalm we're supposed to sing. I slouch a little. Great. I forgot that Sunday morning is Spanish Mass, which means I have to pay extra attention in order to keep up with everything the priest is saying.

I sit in silence while my thoughts run wild. I turn back to Gus again. Every time I do, Abuela gives me stink eye.

Keeping still in church is the hardest thing to do. When I was younger, I got to draw or play with my LEGOs. But after my First Communion, Abuela said I have an agreement with God to pay attention. Does she know how hard it is to stay focused when there are a million words swirling in the air? And in Spanish?

After Mass, Abuela invites Gus's family over for lunch. We all walk to our cars. I don't ask to go with the Sánchez family like I do sometimes, because I can tell Gus is still mad at me. When we get home and open the door, my dad has a look on his face like someone just ran over his foot with a bicycle.

"I thought we could use the company," Abuela says, smiling.

Papi tenses up but remains silent. Gus's dad senses the tension and says that maybe they should plan to visit another weekend.

"Mejor, otra semana," Señor Orestes tells Abuela.

Abuela tries to convince everyone that it's perfectly fine to have a little lunch then to go home, but Señor Orestes insists.

"Gracias, Doña Aurelia," he says. "Pero hay que hacer mandados hoy. I'll see you around, T."

My dad nods without looking up.

"Sí, gracias, Aurelia, muy amable," Gus's mom thanks Abuela for the kind offer while holding a sleeping Daniela.

Abuela relents and agrees to host a barbeque after church next weekend. This weekend is barely over and she's already planning a church thing for *next* weekend. Abuela really wants to make God happy, I guess.

She steps outside and waves as Gus's family drives off.

She turns back to the living room and glares at my dad.

"Antonio," she says. "That was very rude."

Papi gets up and moves closer to Abuela.

"I told you not to spring people on me like that, Mami. Even if it's great people like the Sánchez family."

Abuela tells my dad that he needs to start going out more and socializing. She says he needs to at least go to church. I can see Papi tuning out. He walks back to the sofa and sinks into it. He shakes his head in frustration while Abuela goes to the kitchen.

Papi offers me the seat next to him. I'm not sure if it's a good idea, since he's not in the best mood, but I walk over and sit anyway. Abuela stomps around in the kitchen. I hear the faucet running and plates clanging against silverware.

"We have a dishwasher, Mami!" Dad yells. "Geez, I don't remember her being like this," he says to me. "This is too much."

"I know," I reply. "Maybe she's stressed with Mami gone or maybe she's worried about y—" I stop myself. I don't want to tell him that maybe he's the problem. Maybe we all are.

My dad sets his big arm across the sofa. He takes the

remote control and starts flipping through channels.

"Any suggestions?" he asks.

"How about *Rock My Wreck*?" I say. It's a car show about a bunch of guys who fix junk cars.

Papi lets out a laugh and the room revs to life. "I love that show," he says.

"Yeah, me too."

He clicks on the guide and searches for the channel.

"It's two-forty-two," I tell him. "That's an on-demand channel. It's in the saved folder."

He hands me the remote so I can find the show.

"There's a new fixer on the team now," I tell him. "Her name is Shirley. She's awesome."

"I bet," he says.

We press play and watch quietly together. I can see Abuela's reflection on the television screen. She's standing in the dining room, watching us without saying a word. My dad doesn't notice, but I do.

# CHAPTER NINETEEN

At school the next day, Mr. Richt asks if anyone would like to update the class on their project.

"I warned you I'd do this," he says. "Would anyone care to share what they've been up to?"

I almost never raise my hand in class, but I have so much to share.

"Yes, Miss Torres. Take it away!"

I tell the class all the other stuff I've learned while working on this project. About the ACLU, about anti-immigration laws. I tell them that my mom says the biggest thing people can do when they turn eighteen is to register to vote, and fight for that right even though some lawmakers make it hard for everyone. Because voting decides a lot of things in a person's life, like where they can live and where they can go to school.

"But that's not enough," I say, feeling charged up.

"We're kids, but that doesn't mean we have to stay silent and wait till we're old enough to vote. We can speak up and help right now. Like my mom says, we need to look out for one another."

It all spills out at once.

"What in the world? That's not a *tourism guide!*" Clarissa interrupts. "Where did you get all that information? You didn't find that junk in the *library*."

"It's not junk," Gus says. "It's hidden information. Like a monster under your bed."

"You and your stupid monsters, Gustavo. Why don't you just keep quiet for once?"

"I'm not going to keep quiet, Clarissa. You're the one cutting people off all the time."

Mr. Richt gets up from his seat. "Hey, let's get back on track, you two. And, Miss Anderson, watch your language, you understand?"

Clarissa glares then busies herself by organizing her pens by size and color.

Mr. Richt moves toward me. "Do you have your sources, Miss Torres?"

I pause for a second before nodding.

"They're on my phone."

"You can't use the Internet!" Clarissa blurts out.

"I didn't! I mean, most of my research is from the library."

Mr. Richt asks me to get my phone from my locker. I take it out to show him my list of folders in the notes app.

"This is thorough, Miss Torres, but these are websites."

"See? She can't use those!" Clarissa shouts.

"No, she can't," Mr. Richt says. "These books and these interviews, yes. I bet you can find some of this other information, and more, by going to city hall."

"Mr. Richt—" I start, but he doesn't let me finish.

"I'm sure you'll continue to find things within the parameters of my rules, right?"

"I guess so," I tell him. Out of the corner of my eye, I catch Clarissa smirking.

So is Mr. Richt allowing me to use the information I found or not?

"Anybody else have addendums to their projects or other expansive updates like Miss Torres?"

"Mr. Richt!" Jay shouts. "It's not nice to call students dumb dumbs!"

The class laughs, and Jay puts his hand up for Richie to high-five him. Richie ignores him and Jay scans awkwardly around before putting his hand back down. Richie then raises his hand to ask a question.

"Yes, Mr. Barre?"

"Actually, Mr. Richt, I . . . I kind of want to change my topic if that's okay."

"To what?"

"Well, I want to do more of a historical tourism guide, to find out more about what Merryville was like during the Civil Rights era," Richie says.

Mr. Richt nods for Richie to continue.

"Hey," Jay says, angling at Richie. "What do you care about *that* for?"

"I started my tour at the rec center, and I learned that it used to be a meeting place for organizers in the sixties. I want to know more about that."

"But you're not black, dude."

"So? That doesn't mean I shouldn't learn about it." Pretty soon, almost everyone in class asks to change their project or add more to it.

Chinh raises his hand.

"Go ahead, Mr. Nguyen."

"I'll work with Jay," he says.

"Wait, what?" Jay is totally shocked.

"But," Chinh continues, "I want to focus on football head injuries and safe measures to take when playing."

"What?!" Jay blurts out. "Chinh, what kind of tourism guide is *that*?"

"'*Tourism*,'" Chinh says, reading from his phone. "By definition, it's 'the commercial organization and operation of vacations and visits to places of interest.' The football field is a commercial place of interest, and a tour guide can offer more information than just how it was built."

Jay is silent for a moment before he barks, "No way! I'll think of my own project, Mr. Richt."

"Very well," Mr. Richt says. "Mr. Nguyen, excellent choice for a project."

"Thank you, sir."

"Now put your phone away before I confiscate it."

Chinh quickly shoves his phone into his backpack and puts his hands on his desk.

"In the locker, Mr. Nguyen. Phone in the locker."

"Yes, sir," Chinh says. He pulls the phone out and stares at it lovingly like a baby. "I'll see you later, precious," he says, kissing the screen.

Gus shakes his head and we make eye contact before he turns away. I really wish he would talk to me.

Lacey jumps in and says she's going to add information on women performers to her tour.

"Did you know that a woman is responsible for the theater in town? She was one of the first female business owners in Merryville. I didn't know that. I think I want to add a musical component for my visitors too."

"Can I dump my project and join up with Lacey?" Jeff asks while raising his hand.

"If Miss Roberts agrees, I don't see any problem with it."

"Oh, totally!" Lacey gives Jeff a thumbs-up.

"Duet tours!" they sing out in unison.

"Uh, Lacey," Clarissa says. She looks like she ate a rotten peach. "You said at my party that you were thinking about working with me."

"Well, yeah, but I like this project more, Clarissa. I'm sorry."

"Fine," Clarissa says. "I'll change my project too, Mr. Richt."

"Go ahead, Miss Anderson."

"I want to change mine to how great Merryville's schools are and how they don't need more students. Especially from Park View."

She sounds like a dusty old car muffler. And like a

muffler, her words leave a cloud of noxious gas in the air. A few students look genuinely shocked. But a few also nod in agreement.

"What do you propose that tour to be, Miss Anderson?"

"Well, I'd take visitors to each school in Merryville. I'd give them a brochure showing how clean and nice Merryville is and what would happen if the schools take in students from Park View. You said it could be anything that talks about visiting a place, right, Mr. Richt?"

"I did," Mr. Richt says. It's like Clarissa is testing his patience.

I can't believe she wants to argue for closing schools to students from other areas! She won't make eye contact with me.

"The point I want to make with these projects," Mr. Richt says, "is that you should take risks, challenge your-selves. Disagreeing is okay as long as you support your argument, with facts."

It's hard to focus for the rest of class. I'm excited and furious at the same time. When the bell rings, I slip out quick. I don't really want to talk to anyone right now.

After math class, Ms. Brennen pulls me to the side and hands me my math grade.

"I can give you a chance to retake the test, Emilia. But please study next time."

There's a gigantic D in bloodred marker across the top of my test. If my mom found out I got a D, I think she would fly back on the next plane to annihilate me.

"Promise me you'll study for the retest?"

"Yes," I say. "I'm sorry, Ms. Brennen."

"It's okay, Emilia. I know your mom was gone last week and your daddy just got back. Make sure you study, though, okay?"

"I will," I say.

I thank Ms. Brennen and head out to the hallway. When I step outside, I can hear Gus before I see him, and it gives me the shivers. He's in a full-blown argument with Clarissa. Students stand around them as they bark at each other and say things that are awful.

Clarissa yells at Gus that he has no right to talk to her this way.

"You're not even from here!" she barks.

"I'm from Alabama!" Gus shouts back. "But I live here now!"

"Nobody asked you to move, though!"

At first, I can't believe Clarissa says these things. Actually, that's not exactly true. She's always been cold to Gus. But this is deep-freezer cold.

"Why does he need your permission, Clarissa?" I finally say. The crowd of kids turns to me and I step back a little. I don't like all this attention.

"Stay out of it, Emi Rose," Clarissa says. "Why are *you* suddenly interested in immigration and laws and school districts? You're spreading lies about your *home*. Who's going to want to come visit the place you describe? You should fail your project."

"Everything I said is true, Clarissa," I say through gritted teeth. "I can send you the links—"

"It's not like any of that affects you or anything. You were born here. You speak English properly, not like Gustavo. You're one of *us*, Emi Rose. You're betraying your neighbors. It's sad."

Clarissa's words electrocute me. It's a fast, hot jolt to the skin followed by an intense sting. I got zapped for real when I was around ten, a few weeks after Gus had moved to Merryville. There was a loose wire in the garage and I picked it up. Señor Orestes rushed over just in time to

246

help me. But I remember the feeling—the vibration in my head, like an aftershock.

I try to find anything to get me out of this hallway, but I'm dizzy and I can hardly hear over the arguing. Gus mouths something to me, but I don't respond. Clarissa continues to yell at him. And that gets other students snapping at each other. They're on both sides of me and I'm caught in the middle, blocked from the hallway so I can't run away. Mr. Richt appears with a few other teachers to break up the arguing. He puts his hands up and calls for calm. I take my backpack and leave the second I have an opening, without saying anything to Gus or Clarissa.

When I get far enough away, I stop next to the water fountain. The water shoots out long streams. I have to step back a little or I'll get soaked. Everything will get soaked.

# CHAPTER TWENTY

When I get home after sitting in the woods on a tree stump to think, I hear the three words I hate more than anything else in the world.

"Hay que limpiar," Abuela says. "A clean house will make your papi happy. Then we can cook something nice for him."

"All he does is sit on the sofa or go to his room," I reply. "I don't think he cares what the rest of the house is like."

"He's going through a lot, mi'ja. It's up and down. We have to be patient."

I'm tired of hearing that I need to be more patient with everything.

Abuela takes out the mop and broom and leans them against the wall. Then she turns on the radio to La Nueva Mega, a radio station based out of Atlanta. Abuela really needs to learn how to read a room. Now is not the time for Latin pop songs.

"It's always good to learn how to clean up after yourself," she says, wiggling her hips. "And, of course, to cook."

"I know how to cook, Abuela."

"Well, I haven't given you my secret picadillo recipe yet," she says. "That used to be your father's favorite when he was your age."

She starts sweeping and dusting around the dining room table.

"Pour the Mistolín into the bucket," she says, pointing to the floor cleaner that smells like lavender and really tart limes.

I dip the mop in and drag it across the floor like it's a lazy dance partner. Abuela doesn't seem to notice, because she moves from sweeping to dusting to setting the table at a pace that's like she drank twenty cafés con leche.

She pauses to look at me and takes the mop from my hands.

"Mi'ja," she says. "You're not mopping at all. ¡Dale con gusto!"

Mom, Abuela, and I used to do the chores around the house together. I would sweep; Mom would do the laundry. Now Abuela is telling me to help her do everything while my dad sits upstairs watching television? It's ridiculous.

"Abuela," I say. "Papi should be down here helping us clean."

"Mi'ja, your father is recovering. He needs time. Oh, and look at your socks," she comments.

I have one bright-orange-and-yellow sock on my left foot and one blue with white polka dots on the other. I've had them on since this morning. Why do I need matching socks to clean the house?

"I like it," I say, admiring them.

Abuela exhales and shakes her head. "Bueno," she says, "let's go make the picadillo with arroz y frijoles negros."

"I hate black beans, Abuela."

"Are you not feeling well?" Abuela checks my forehead for a fever. "What kind of person doesn't like frijoles negros?"

"I know," I say, feeling irritated. "I guess I'm a bad Cuban. I feel like getting bánh mì instead."

"¿Cómo que *bánh mì*?" she asks, tilting her head. "You're not Vietnamese."

"That doesn't mean I can't like Vietnamese food. I love that place in Cartersville we went to with Mom a few months ago."

"A mi no me gustó," she says. "Too spicy."

"Well, *I* think it's delicious."

"Emilia, that place is thirty minutes away. We're not going to go eat that right now. Vamos, let's prep for dinner."

I clench my jaw and march angrily to the kitchen.


At dinner, Abuela puts out the picadillo. We cut little potatoes and fry them into crispy cubes and add them to the ground beef and olives. There's a tray of black beans and rice, but I just move the beans to the side.

My dad eats in silence while Abuela goes on and on about how we cleaned the house and made the meal. She asks my dad how he's feeling and if he likes the food and blah, blah, blah.

"Y Emilia and I are going to go to Atlanta over the weekend to maybe look for dresses," Abuela tells my dad, who is still checked out.

"You know, Emilia," Abuela says. "I've been thinking. Maybe it's a good thing you haven't gone to the woods with Gustavo in a few days. You need to help me around the house more. You're becoming a señorita and that comes with responsibilities."

I've had it. No más.

"Abuela, what is wrong with you?!" I say, standing up from the table. "This talk about being 'una mujercita' and planning my quinceañera and now you're telling me that I shouldn't hang out with Gus. Well, guess what?! I don't like to clean, and I don't want to cook and I'm fine with my socks and church can be boring even if I made a promise to God! And I. Like. Spicy! Gah, just leave me alone already!"

Oh no. The Coke bottle with lemon juice has officially exploded.

"And *you*," I tell my dad as my anger surges. "Papi, you just want to work on that Shelby, Green Hornet, whatever you call it, and watch TV. You don't even take a second to explain *why*? *Why* didn't you respond to my videos? You could have sent at least *one* note. At least told me *one time* that you liked them, hated them, *anything*. But you didn't. And now when I ask you, you just get upset. Well, you know what, Papi?"

Tears stream down my face. It's slick, like the rain that makes it hard for tires to get traction on a road.

"You know what?" I repeat, wiping my face. "I don't care anymore, Papi. I don't care that you didn't respond or that you don't want to talk or that you won't even think about getting some help. You leave me alone too!"

I take off, dragging my napkin halfway to the base of

the stairs before it falls to the floor. I run to my room and instead of diving into my pillow, I pace around with my jaw clenched and my hands balled into fists. I'm so sick of everything and everyone!

I grab my phone to open my puzzle app. I want to do the ten-thousand-piece puzzle and not come out of my room until I'm done.

Before I open the app, I see an unread text. Mom has sent me a message.

Mom: Big News!!! Call you soon!!!

My phone rings and I answer it.

"Hi, Mami."

"Hey, mi amor! How are you? You okay? You sound upset."

"It's nothing. Abuela is being *super*-annoying. And I yelled at Papi and I don't know. When are you coming home?"

"I'm so sorry, honey. I'll be home Thursday."

"Everything is a mess right now."

"We'll talk through it, okay? Don't worry."

My mom says that because she doesn't know the whole story.

"You should talk to Gus. How's he doing?"

"We haven't spoken in a few days. He's mad at me. Then he got into a big fight with Clarissa at school today and she said something that was really hurtful, but I don't even know what to think about it."

"What did she say?"

"She said that my project is nothing but lies and that talking bad about Merryville is like I'm betraying my neighbors. I froze and didn't say anything, and Gus watched me like he was totally over our friendship."

"Aye, esa niña. I'm going to have a talk with her mother." I hear Mom exhale loudly. "I'm sorry you're dealing with all that, mi amor. I'll also call Mrs. Jenk—"

"Mami! I don't want you calling Clarissa's mom or Mrs. Jenkins. There are other kids who could use some help too. Like Barry, who seems to be struggling like me, but nobody cares. Besides, how can other students see Mrs. Jenkins if you make me talk to her all her time? There are problems bigger than mine that need attention."

All I hear is the hum of the phone under the silence. Mom takes another deep breath and continues. "Okay, mi amor. You're right. *Every* student should get the same amount of help, and there are other important things that need attention. Geez, I leave for a few days and you grow so much. You're not going to need me soon."

"Of course I'm going to need you, Mom," I say, fidgeting with my puzzle app.

"So, how about some good news?"

I start to feel nervous again, and I don't know why.

"I just had an *amazing* meeting with a company. . . ."

"Yeah?"

"Not only do they want to develop my app, they want to hire me to work full-time! Isn't that incredible? I haven't said yes, but I'm seriously considering. I can't wait to tell you all about it. The Bay Area is *amazing*!"

I put the phone on mute. What is going on right now?

"Emilia, you there? Hello?"

I take the phone off mute.

"Yeah."

"What's wrong?"

What's wrong? What's wrong?! She's just been offered a job in *San Francisco* and she's "seriously considering," that's what's wrong! I've already yelled at Abuela *and* Papi. I just don't have the energy to yell at my mom, too.

"Honey, listen. We'll talk about the details when I'm home. Nothing is set in stone. . . ."

I look at my socks again. I smell the arroz y frijoles and the picadillo downstairs. Nothing is right about any of this. Nothing. My mom says this is the opportunity of her life. She says she'll be able to give me everything she's always wanted to give me.

I don't tell her that the only thing I need is for her to be here. At home. In Merryville. Helping me talk through all these problems. I don't tell her that I don't care about San Francisco.

"Okay, Mom."

That's all I say. The phone is quiet.

"Does that sound like a plan?"

"Yeah. Fine. Bye, Mom."

"A little change might be good for all of us, mi amor."

"For you, maybe. Anyway, I gotta go. I have to study for a math retake."

"Maybe I can help. I have some time now."

"No, I can do it myself. Thanks. Bye."

"Okay? Bye, baby. I love you."

"Bye."

I hang up the phone. I know she feels bad. I could hear it in her voice. After sending every ounce of anger I have inside to the people I love most in this world, I don't even have the energy to cry anymore. I wait awhile to see if my dad or Abuela knocks or comes into my room. But neither of them do. I hardly even hear a footstep.

# CHAPTER TWENTY-ONE

I'm in the office early the next morning, waiting to talk to Mrs. Jenkins about my math test. I'm sitting in a chair next to Principal Andrews's office when I overhear a conversation she's having with Mr. Richt.

"I told you to keep the history project light."

"A tourism guide is light," Mr. Richt says.

"Come on, Mike. You encouraged them to go off course."

"I'm proud of them," he says. "Emilia especially. That kid sparked a great discussion and the entire class followed her lead."

My heart skips a few beats. Overhearing your favorite teacher say they're proud of you feels really good.

"Many parents have called to complain saying the project is too controversial. That it's causing their kids to act out disrespectfully."

"They are gathering, analyzing, and synthesizing information related to social studies topics and applying that information to contemporary problems."

"I appreciate you adhering to school district standards, Mike," Principal Andrews tells Mr. Richt, "and the creative nature of the project. But students fighting in the hallways and yelling at each other is not how they should process information. Come up with something else. Something *not controversial*, okay? I don't want to have to write you up again."

"Yes, ma'am."

Mr. Richt doesn't argue further. He doesn't say much more, actually. Like he's just given up. Mr. Richt leaves the room looking defeated. When he walks past me, he just gives me a weak smile. A few minutes later Mrs. Jenkins calls me into her office to talk.

"Hey there, Emilia." She tells me that some teachers have said I was extra distracted in class last week. I mostly stay quiet. My brain is still exhausted.

"Your mom will be home soon," she says. "I'm sure she'll get you back on track."

I think about the train tracks in town. How they run through Merryville, most times without stopping. Would anyone riding those trains know anything about what goes on here? Would they bother to look for Park View if they visited—get to know the people who help make this place so vibrant? Would they bother to find out?

"Emilia, are you okay?"

"Yes," I say, and ask to be excused.

"Sure."

Before I leave, I say, "Mrs. Jenkins?"

"Yes, Emilia?"

"You should check in with Barry Johnson every once in a while. He's really smart. Actually, there are lots of kids who might need a little attention. Not just me."

I don't wait for her to answer. "Have a nice day," I tell her, closing the door behind me.

Homeroom feels tense and quiet.

I sit down at my desk and watch Gus walk into class. We make eye contact and then he moves over to his locker to put away his things. When he sits down, I offer a hello.

"Hi," he says, sounding distant.

"I hate everything that's happened," I tell him.

"Yeah."

"Like a horror movie."

"It's not a horror movie, Emilia. It's real life."

"I'm sorry for Clarissa's party, Gus."

"Do you have any idea what happened that night?" he asks. "My apá stays in town so he can pick me up from Clarissa's house. And on the way back, we got stopped by a cop!"

My heart drops to my knees. I immediately think about the articles I read.

"They said my dad was speeding, pero no era cierto. Luckily, we had our documentation with us ¿pero si no? And Barry hasn't spoken to me since because I bailed on our movie night and storyboarding."

I can't believe all of that happened because I was too distracted with my own stuff.

"I told you I didn't want to go to Clarissa's stupid party."

His voice gets higher than I've ever heard it.

"And yesterday—you just left! You didn't even stick around to put Clarissa in her place. I'm starting to think she's right. Maybe you don't understand."

His words sting. It's like a sunburn in the middle of summer and I have no sunscreen or aloe to cool it down.

After the Pledge of Allegiance, moment of silence, and morning announcements, Mr. Richt stands up from his desk to get everyone's attention. Homeroom is over and he's trying to start first-period social studies.

"Listen up, folks. We're going to switch gears. I know you were all looking forward to presenting your projects, but there's been a change in the curriculum."

Everyone groans.

"So, no more project?" Richie asks.

"Actually, we're just going to swap topics," Mr. Richt says. "Instead of the individual tourism guides, I'd like you all to attend the school board meeting on Thursday, after which we can discuss democracy."

"Mr. Richt," Clarissa starts up. "I mean, I thought the project was just canceled?"

"The old one is canceled," he says. "But they can't stop us from observing and discussing the democratic process. You should all attend and report back on Friday with your thoughts."

The class seems to have mixed feelings about this new project. A few students say we shouldn't have to do anything now. Others say they worked really hard on their projects already.

"I know you have," Mr. Richt says. "But my hands are tied. I am required to oblige, but I am also required to teach you and I have elected to do so in this manner. Okay?"

A few students move in their seats, but no one says anything. Mr. Richt continues his lesson and I make sure to keep pace, jotting down notes quickly while looking up and trying to find the right moment to talk to Gus. Mr. Richt pauses to write something on the board. I lean forward and whisper.

"Gus, I just want to say that I'm so sorry. That's it. No excuses."

"Thanks . . ." he says, not turning around. "But I just need some space, Emilia. Okay?"

Mr. Richt continues his lesson, but I keep trying with Gus. I drop my pencil in front of his desk and he picks it up and turns around. We watch each other for a moment.

"Look, I know I don't know everything. But I want to keep learning. To do better. That's gotta count for something."

He hands me the pencil.

"And I *do* understand, Gus. I might be friends with Clarissa, but that doesn't automatically mean that I think like her. That's unfair, too. But I promise I'm not going to sit around quietly anymore, especially when I learn that things are wrong. No más. I'm keeping this *Millennium Falcon* in hyperdrive, Gus Sánchez." I take the pencil from him and *tap-tap-tap* it on my desk. "I'm ready for whatever galactic battle awaits us."

Gus looks at me and softens. "That's real, Emilia Torres."

"¿Amigos por siempre?" I ask.

"So, am I Chewbacca on this *Millennium Falcon* of yours?"

"Nah," I say. "Let's make our own Star Wars story. Together. If you want to."

"Órale," he says.

"I will always be here for you, Gus. And I really am sorry I haven't been doing a good job of that lately."

"I know it's been hard with your dad," Gus says.

"It has. But I don't want to use that as an excuse."

After social studies, we walk together to Gus's math class, even though mine is the opposite way.

"I'm going to talk to Principal Andrews," Gus says. "I should be in honors classes."

"You should."

We start our special handshake before we head off.

"Let's meet up after school," he says.

"Órale!" I holler back, and he laughs.

When I drop off Gus, I think about all the things we still have to talk about. I honestly can't wait to get started.

After school, Gus and I walk down a trail until we come across a fork. I tell him that I'm worried about talking to Abuela.

"It's family, you know?" he says. "It will work out eventually."

"Yeah. You're right. Hey, are you still going to finish your movie even though the project is canceled?"

"I don't know," he says. "Maybe I can use my talents for more serious things."

"But monster movies can say serious things. Like Guillermo del Toro, remember?"

"You're right. He really likes to hold up a mirror to society. At least that's what all the critics seem to say."

I stop in my tracks because what Gus says gives me an idea.

"That's perfect! Let's hold a mirror to the town. I mean, a camera."

"What?" Gus asks.

"People here are so upset about this school board vote," I explain. "Let's film interviews with Park View residents and students about their opinions on the redistricting. We can't vote, but we can at least help Park View be heard and provide more information to the school board members who *do* vote."

"Yeah!" Gus is totally fired up. "No one has bothered to ask Park View students and parents what they think. How do we know they even want to come to our school?"

"Exactly."

Gus beams. "Do you think Mr. Richt will let us?" he asks.

"I mean, he didn't say we couldn't have partners, right?"

"Very true," Gus replies. "Let's do it!"

We get to the auto shop, and I spot Abuela's bun through the little office window. Gus tells me he'll hang out with his dad while I talk to her.

"She'll listen. She's tough, but she loves you."

That makes me feel better.

I take a deep breath and walk over to the door. The AC hits me first. Abuela's wearing her reading glasses as she fills out some paperwork.

"Hola, mi'ja," she says, without an ounce of anger in her voice. She gets up.

"Abuela, can we talk?"

She moves to the door and walks through it, leaving me in the office by myself. So much for trying to make amends. She heads to her truck and hops in. The air-conditioning blasts inside the office. I seriously can't believe she's doing this!

I step outside and let the warm air wash over me. Abuela is fidgeting with the radio knobs in the truck. I try to make eye contact with her, but she ignores me.

Agustín comes out of one of the stalls, carrying two empty gallons of synthetic oil. I wave, and he nods.

"Hola, Emilia," he says, tossing the gallons in the recycling.

"Hey, Agustín."

"How's it going?"

"Good, wild day at school. Wild couple of weeks, actually."

"Yeah," he says, shifting the bill of his baseball cap to the other side. "You going to the school board meeting?"

"Oh yeah," I tell him. "Gus and I are going to film it."

"Awesome."

"How do you feel about it?"

"Well, my little sister might have to move to a new school next year, two years before she graduates high school, so, no, I'm not down."

"Yeah, high school students shouldn't have to move to a new school right before they graduate."

"And the selection has nothing to do with choice. Somebody decides for us."

Gus steps outside and watches me talk to Agustín.

"Hey, Gus?" I yell out.

"Yeah?"

"I think we have our first interview." Agustín nods like he's ready to speak his mind. Gus rushes over with his video camera and starts shooting.

"Agustín Reyes," I say just to the side of the camera. "Can you tell us how you feel about the pending school redistricting that will affect students in both Merryville *and* Park View schools?"

Agustín lifts his cap. He stares directly at the camera and begins talking.

Gus leans over.

"He is so action-hero cool," he whispers while we film

Agustín. I turn around to find Abuela watching me from inside her truck.

She's lowered the window and nods for me to join her inside.

"¿Quieres ir conmigo?" she asks.

I look over to Gus.

"Go," he says. "I got this."

I hop in and Abuela backs up out of the shop. We drive in silence through the streets. I have no idea where we're going.

It's quiet in town. The only sound in the truck is salsa music from the radio, tuned low.

"Me encanta esta canción," she says.

"It's a good song."

We drive down Main Street toward the train tracks, and the woods come into view.

"I never had a quinceañera," she offers.

"Wait, really?"

"We left Cuba when I was a little girl, not too much younger than you."

Abuela says she and her family lived in a factory town called Hershey, Cuba.

"Like the chocolate company?"

"Sí," she says. "There was one in Cuba. When the factory closed, we came to the United States."

Abuela says that her dad tried to find work in factory towns all over the Northeast. They would pack up their things to follow whatever job was available.

"He didn't speak much English, but he worked hard. Eventually we ended up living right here."

"Abuela, did you know Sara J. González?"

"No, ¿quién es?"

"She was a business owner from Cuba who lived in Atlanta and fought for the rights of people who weren't born in this country and work here. She helped them settle and made them feel welcome."

Abuela says she hasn't heard of her. "Pero me interesa saber más."

"I want to learn more about her life too, like, at what point did she become an activist? Did you know there's a park named after her? It's in Atlanta."

"Maybe we can go and visit it," Abuela says. "That will be nice, ¿no?"

"Yeah, as long as you don't trick me into going dress shopping again."

"Pero, Emilia, eventually you have to let me plan your quinceañera."

"We'll see, Abuela."

Abuela drives below the overpass.

"So, you moved to Merryville after that?" I ask.

"Not quite."

She drives farther and farther away from Main Street. We pass the parking lot of Don Carlos's Grocery Latino and the sign for the Mexican restaurant attached to Don Carlos's store and the Vietnamese nail and hair salon.

"The best years of my teens were when I lived in Park View."

We end up at a tiny one-story house sandwiched between two other little houses. The paint has peeled off and the lawn is patchy. There's an old swing on a large beech tree to the side.

Abuela parks the truck and stares at the house. "I was fifteen when we moved here."

"Really?"

"It was the first house we lived in for more than two years. I planned my quince all year long, but my mother got very sick. Y cuando Mami murió, nos mudamos otra vez."

"I didn't know that."

"Emilia, when you were born, I thanked God for giving me the treasure of my life."

"Thank you, Abuela," I start. "But if you loved living here in Park View as a kid, and you shop here, and most of the friends you hang out with are here, why did you move to Merryville and why do you only remind me of my European ancestors?"

Abuela opens her mouth like she wants to say something, but nothing comes out.

"Park View is part of your history, Abuela, and Mami says we should recognize *every part* of who we are."

Abuela opens her mouth to say something two more times. On the third try, I guess she figures out what she wants to say.

"Emilia, I just want you to avoid the things I endured. I don't want you to suffer like I did, mi'ja."

"What do you mean, Abuela?"

"After my father passed away, I ended up living in Forsyth County," she says. "Not too far from here. I met your abuelo at a church event. He was un flaco with big ears and had the greatest laugh in the entire world."

I smile, reminded of the pictures of my abuelo that are sprinkled throughout our living room.

"When your father was born, we wanted a stable home for him to grow up in. We saved money, bought our house, and saved more money to buy the auto shop."

The song on the radio changes and so does Abuela's face.

"Then your abuelo got sick and people kept trying to buy the place because they didn't think a woman, much less a Cuban woman, could run the only auto shop in town."

"Why would anyone think that?"

"Because people can be ignorant, Emilia."

"What did you do?"

"I tried to make friends with everyone in town. I hosted barbecues, organized church events, went to parades, and cheered for the football team. At home, I could play my music, cook my picadillo, y pude expresarme de cualquiera manera. But outside, I was careful. I know you know. Think about what you learned with your project."

All this time, I thought Abuela was disappointed in me.

"Abuela," I say, "but after everything you've been through, why would you want to hide?"

She lifts her brow.

"Your dad wasn't afraid to find work when he came here from Cuba and didn't speak English."

She lets out a laugh that I think surprises her.

"You are very smart, Emilia."

"Abuela, I don't want to hide or erase parts of myself. Especially the parts I got from Mami. That makes me feel bad."

Abuela grips the wheel tightly in silence. Finally she turns to me.

"Okay, mi amor. No more hiding anything. Okay?"

I nod.

"I'm sorry I yelled at you, Abuela."

"You needed to get that out," she tells me. "I understand. Pero no me faltes el respeto, okay? Sigo siendo tu abuela."

"Okay," I tell her. I understand that I shouldn't disrespect her by yelling.

"Talk to me," she says. "I reserve the right not to listen, but I promise I will hear you."

I'm not sure what she means, but I decide to accept it anyway. It's baby steps with Abuela. "Okay, deal."

Abuela starts the truck up again and we pass Don Carlos's.

"Don Felix seems to like you," I say.

Abuela practically turns into a tomato.

"¡Aye, niña! ¿Cómo vas a decir eso?"

"I mean, he gives you free samples, you two are always smiling at each other when we go to the store, and you invite him to sit with us at church sometimes. He's cute, in that grandfatherly way."

"He is a very kind man. And he has a very well-groomed mustache."

"Is that your thing, Abuela? Mustaches?"

"¿Qué?" Abuela says. I think she was daydreaming of Don Felix's mustache. "No! Enough talk about this!"

I can't help but giggle as we drive back to the auto shop.

"You must be excited that your mother is coming home soon," she says.

"Why do you two always fight?"

"Supongo que we're more similar than we'd like to admit."

"Stubborn and overprotective?"

"Oyeme, no te pases."

"What? It's true."

Abuela laughs. When we return to the shop, Gus is

showing his dad the camera. Señor Orestes keeps opening the flap to look at the screen.

"You should go talk to your father," Abuela says, parking the truck.

"Is he super-angry?"

"He was sad, but he's fine now. I think he wanted to give you some space. He's at home if you want to see to him."

"Not yet," I say.

I'm not ready to talk to my dad.

I hop out of the car and rush over to Gus.

"He wants me to film him replacing a tire, but he keeps insisting I use the screen so he can see himself while he works."

"I didn't take your dad for a movie star diva."

"I regret ever telling him that I could put him on YouTube. Seriously."

Abuela waves as somebody pulls into the shop. She is tough. Strong. Stubborn. Overly protective. But she's my abuela. I wouldn't want her any other way.

# CHAPTER TWENTY-TWO

The day after the school board meeting, homeroom is buzzing with energy. It seems like everyone showed up, and we're all ready to talk about it. Mr. Richt didn't require his other classes to attend—just us. He said Principal Andrews came to a compromise where we could go (as long as we were quiet and saved the discussion for class), but not the entire sixth grade. Mr. Richt had no choice but to agree.

I watch as Gus and Barry talk in the hall before the bell rings. Barry nods quietly as Chinh steps in and puts his arms around both Barry and Gus. Gus told me that things haven't been the same with his friends since Clarissa's party. I'm really glad to see them together again.

Once the bell rings, practically the whole class raises their hands to speak.

"Well," Clarissa starts, but Lacey hushes her before Mr. Richt can.

"Clarissa Anderson," Lacey says, "I am tired of you raising your hand and speaking before you're even called on. You always go first, and that isn't fair."

Clarissa opens her mouth, but Jeff Samuels cuts her off.

"Stop interrupting, Clarissa!"

Clarissa waits for Mr. Richt to say something, but he just motions for Lacey to continue. "Go ahead, Miss Roberts," he says. "Miss Anderson, wait your turn."

Lacey explains that the school board meeting felt like a courtroom drama.

"The school board district members were like the judges at the front of the room, listening while everyone spoke their opinions freely."

"That's an excellent point, Miss Roberts. The right to speak openly is a tremendous freedom we enjoy in this country."

"Made me proud to be an American," Lacey says. "Plus, I *loved* the way Mrs. Loretta got up and shushed everyone who was interrupting TJ, the Park View football player. That was awesome."

Mr. Richt nods in agreement.

"We should get that kid!" Jay butts in. "He's huge!

We'd win districts for sure. I'd vote to have the redistricting in that case."

"*We* should *get* that kid?" Chinh argues. "You think he's like a toy to collect? He said he didn't want to move next year because he wants to play on the team his dad coaches, Jay."

"So?" Jay croaks. "This school is way better. We have a better field and better equipment."

"Dude, you really need to stop talking," Richie says. I can tell that Jay is intimidated by Richie right now because he just goes quiet.

"Mr. Richt," Richie continues. "I don't understand how Merryville residents were talking about a 'Park View problem.' I mean, I play ball at the rec center with kids from Park View *and* Merryville."

"That's right," Mr. Richt says. "The rec center is for *everybody* who lives in the city of Merryville."

"I just don't get why people are so upset that a few kids from Park View might come to our school next year," Richie says.

"But not all Park View kids want to come to Merryville, Richie," Lacey adds. "Like TJ."

Barry mumbles something and Mr. Richt asks him to speak up.

"I don't know," Barry starts. "It's hard enough to be noticed with this many kids at Merryville. I feel like some of us might get even more lost."

"We'll look out for each other, B," Gus says. "Right, Emilia?"

I nod and smile at Barry.

When the class goes quiet, Clarissa waves both of her arms in the air. "Mr. Richt, may I speak now?"

"Go ahead, Miss Anderson."

Clarissa stands up and addresses the class like she's running for president or something.

"That's exactly why Merryville schools and Park View schools should stay as they are. Should we deny someone like TJ McMillian the right to stay at his school and play football on the team his daddy coaches?" Clarissa sounds polite, but her words are sharp. "We all live in the community and enjoy the things we have. Why change something that's good? All the redistricting is going to do is create more anger and division among the decent, law-abiding citizens of Merryville. Thank you."

Clarissa sits down and organizes the pencils and markers on her desk. She looks like nothing in the world is bothering her.

That's when Gus and I know it's the right time.

"Ready?"

"Sí," Gus says. I raise my hand and ask if we can present our video.

"Let's see what you have for us, Miss Torres and Mr. Sánchez."

Clarissa's hand shoots up in the air, but Mr. Richt stops her before she can speak.

"You've already had a chance to say your piece, Miss Anderson."

Gus takes out his camera to connect it to the classroom projector. I help by connecting the HDMI cable to the camera.

Mr. Richt turns the lights off, and we press play.

## SCHOOL BOARD REDISTRICTING
## & THE FACES OF MERRYVILLE'S
## PARK VIEW NEIGHBORHOOD:

### Directors
### Gustavo Sánchez & Emilia Torres
### Sixth-Grade Social Studies, Mr. Richt

I face the camera with the Park View playground behind me. Gus pauses to take shots of the surrounding neighborhood. When he gets back to me, he counts down with his fingers so I know when to begin.

> *Me:* Hi! We're here in Park View and we
> wanted to check in on the residents about
> the proposed redistricting and pending vote
> that will impact many students next year.

I walk over to the playground, where Mr. Jackson is sitting on a bench, watching his granddaughters. He kindly agreed to be interviewed for our segment.

*Me:* Hello, Mr. Jackson.

*Mr. Jackson:* Hello there.

*Me:* Could you please let us know a bit about yourself and what your thoughts are on the current school redistricting and the vote coming up?

*Mr. Jackson:* Oh, well, of course. My name is Darren Jackson, and I have lived in Merryville for over forty years. Started my career working at the federal bank and later at the Kmart corporation. Then I retired and worked as a driver on a part-time basis. My wife, Ana Beth, passed away about thirteen months ago, and now I live with my daughter, Sherry; my son-in-law, Mark; and these two young granddaughters right here, Shaneen and Lisa.

*Me:* And what do you think about the school redistricting, Mr. Jackson?

*Mr. Jackson:* You know, I think it's fine. It'd be good, actually, because my daughter keeps fussing about me walking the girls to and from school because she thinks it's pretty far. It's not that far, but if the girls get transferred, it might be good.

Me: Why would it be good, Mr. Jackson?

Mr. Jackson: Well, it'll get my daughter off my back about walking so far, that's for one!

I laugh along with Mr. Jackson. He pauses as Shaneen and Lisa ask him to come back and play.

Mr. Jackson: You know, the thing is, young lady, the actual redistricting stuff is fine, but it hurts when you hear folks talking about kids being dangerous or bad for the community. I mean, do these girls look dangerous to you?

Me: No, sir.

Mr. Jackson: I don't want folks thinking of my granddaughters that way, you understand?

Me: Yes, sir, I do.

Mr. Jackson says goodbye and Gus films him lifting his grandkids onto the swings one by one. Our next interview is with Don Felix. He's wearing his white chef coat and expertly slicing the fat off a juicy red churrasco.

*Don Felix:* Pero nunca tuve hijos, mi'ja.

Don Felix says he loves this community and if he'd had kids, he would've been happy to send them to either one of the schools in Merryville. He was older when he came to Atlanta for work, and never had any children. But he's loved working and living here most of his adult life.

Don Felix helped build Atlanta into the international city it is today, starting way back during the Olympics. Atlanta wouldn't be what it is without his contribution, and neither would Park View. He finishes slicing the skirt steak and places it neatly on the display. Even the meat looks better with Don Felix's perfect slices.

The next interview we film is with Agustín. Gus hardly cuts anything because he declares that "everything Agustín says is awesome."

*Agustín:* Look, I get it. People get scared about change. When I was younger, you should have seen the way people treated my family. Exaggerating their English to make sure we understood. Eyeing us suspiciously the second we walked into a restaurant or a store. Park View doesn't do that. We look out for each other. Sure, we have our quirks, like that guy who keeps chickens and an obnoxious rooster in his yard, and it's hard to play soccer and not send a ball into a windshield with all the cars parked everywhere. But it's home, you know? If everyone in this whole town looked out for one another, like as one big neighborhood, then we'd be stronger. It doesn't all have to be one homogenous population. It can be varied. That's what makes a community great.

Gus pans the camera up and down to show that he agrees with everything Agustín says.

Next we grab footage of Agustín's sister, Amanda, who

lists a whole bunch of statistics, including one about Latino buying power. Agustín was right. She is a genius.

*Amanda:* Georgia residents in immigrant-led households have nineteen point two billion in spending power after tax income. Nineteen. Point. Two. Billion. That was a few years ago. Now it's probably more. So tell me, how are immigrants bad for the economy? We're not a "strain" on resources. Give me a break! Also, we literally live ten blocks away from Main Street. People are talking about the Merryville community as if we're not part of it.

But back to your question. If I'm one of the ones who has to transfer, I'm going to have to start all over. I won't have time to build relationships with teachers at the new school. I'm graduating in two years. How is it going to look on my college applications? I think what we're missing is giving kids a *choice* about their education. Is that a lot to ask for?

We interview several other students, like TJ, who adds that he doesn't want to be separated from his girlfriend.

We also interview Mrs. Loretta. She says she and her kids will benefit from the redistricting because she'll be able to ride into work with them and pick them up at a regular time.

> *Mrs. Loretta:* But this isn't just about me and what's good for my family. It's about what's good for the community. You know, every time I get excited about real change coming that'll benefit *everyone*, some fools go on and make it about themselves. We are *all* part of the same community, are we not? This is just plain silly.

We managed to track down the woman from the restaurant (her name is Alma) and she echoes what Mr. Jackson said.

> *Alma:* People are saying it's going to be dangerous. ¿Peligroso? ¿Para quién?

The last interview is with Gus. He didn't want to. He said a filmmaker speaks through his movies, but he also has a voice that should be heard. The film cuts to the woods as Gus stands near the old gazebo. My hand is wobbly—not steady like his. My feet snap branches as I get close to Gus. It sounds like I'm stepping on a carpet of yucca chips. I ask Gus to tell me what he thinks.

> *Gus:* Sometimes it feels like I'm caught in the middle. I live right on the edge of Park View and Merryville. I go to school in Merryville, but I spend a lot of time in Park View outside of school. I guess that puts me in a place to see both sides. I see how crowded Park View schools are and I see how people from Merryville forget about it. I don't blame the students who don't want to leave, 'cause Park View is really cool. But Merryville has pretty great stuff too. Like the library! I think maybe we all just have to listen to one another more. That's the point of this video, right?

After the final interview, we include footage from the last two weeks. What we notice is that everything we filmed, with the exception of the library, was shot in and around Park View. The woods, the people, the grocery store—it all centered on a place that was being left out of the conversation.

## END VIDEO

# CHAPTER TWENTY-THREE

Mr. Richt flips on the lights. He doesn't show a lot of emotion, but I can tell he's happy by the way he nods.

"You got the file there, Mr. Sánchez?"

"Yes, sir."

"You mind if I post that video to the Merryville Middle YouTube channel?"

"Seriously?"

We're shocked.

"I thought we were just supposed to watch the meeting and take notes," Clarissa says.

"They were there," Mr. Richt says. "And they decided to contribute to the class discussion with a video. All within the *rules*."

"Why do you want to post it, Mr. Richt?" I ask.

"Our community should have access to this information and these stories."

"I'm going to share this video," Richie says.

Lacey agrees and says she's going to tell her mom, who works at the local news station.

"Nice job, G," Barry says.

"We have to be active participants in what goes on in our community," Mr. Richt says. "I'm proud of all of you for participating in this discussion."


When the bell rings, my focus is razor sharp. It's like I can see everything in slow motion.

I tell Gus I'll catch up with him later. I have to retake my math test. When I get to the classroom, Barry is also retaking a test.

"Hey, Barry!"

"What's up, Emi? Are you retaking too? Ms. Brennen said I could have more time to finish."

"It totally helps, right?"

"Yeah. I get nervous when I see the whole class finishing before me."

"I know exactly what you mean."

We sit quietly. No pressure.

When I'm finished, Ms. Brennen grades it right there in front of me.

"B-plus," she says. "Nice improvement, Emilia."

"Thank you for letting me retake it, Ms. Brennen."

"We all deserve a second chance now and again, right?"

Barry gives me a thumbs-up before continuing his work.

"Take as much time as you need, Barry," Ms. Brennen says.


After lunch, I bump into Clarissa in the hall.

"I'm just never going to understand why you would want to be on that side of the fight," she says.

"There doesn't have to be a fight or sides if you don't want there to be, Clarissa."

There's a moment of silence between us. Clarissa fidgets with her bracelet and I notice the charm on it she's had since we were kids.

"First grade was so hard," I say, pointing to her charm. "I remember when you got pulled out of class to hear the news about your dad."

Clarissa continues to play with her bracelet.

"You didn't return that day or the rest of the week. My papi was on one of his first tours, and I realized in that moment that I could've been the one who got asked to go to the principal's office to hear the thing you never want to hear."

Clarissa's lips quiver, but she still doesn't say anything. For once, she just listens, so I continue.

"When you came back, you looked like you were lost in the woods without any sense of how to come home."

Clarissa nods. Tears stream steadily down her face.

"And we started talking to each other about random things, like what was the best ice cream flavor at Jimmy's Diner or how many hot dogs we could eat in one sitting."

Her lips curl up, but her expression is still mostly sad.

"Then you began to open up," I say. "Every time you talked about your dad, I became scared but also relieved that my dad was still out there."

"Yeah," she says.

"I don't hate you, Clarissa," I tell her.

"I considered you my friend, Emi Rose."

"Well," I say, "I'll always thank you for those memories."

"Me too," she says. "But I still don't agree with you." She hesitates for a moment, like she's going to say something else. But instead she turns around to leave.

"Oh, and, Clarissa?" I say loudly as she walks in the opposite direction.

"Yeah?"

"My name is *Emilia Rosa*."

# CHAPTER TWENTY-FOUR

It's hard to muster the energy, but my family decides to attend a small festival that's happening in town over the weekend. Mami has been home for a few days and that's what she wants to do. The festival celebrates the anniversary of when the railroad was built over seventy-five years ago.

"I read at the library about how towns used to be divided by train tracks."

"Yeah?" Papi says to me.

"Living on one side could mean a person was 'on the wrong side of the tracks.' Like they weren't as good as the people living on the 'right' side."

"No me gusta ese dicho." Abuela does not care for that phrase.

"Neither do I," I say. "The only 'wrong side' is the side where people don't care about one another."

Mami squeezes my hand and Papi puts his arm over my shoulders.

"What do you think?" Papi asks.

"I think we got a fighter," Mami says, gently nudging me into Papi.

"¡Mira!" Abuela points to a food truck on the corner. The side says MI'PANA, and it has a picture of something that looks an awful lot like a hamburger, but it's actually a burger with a juicy chorizo patty, manchego cheese, lettuce, and tomato. At the window, I see Don Carlos taking orders while Don Felix cooks. He waves at us and Abuela turns as red as the meat in Don Felix's display case.

Farther down the street, Barry's dad cooks up barbecue at a booth. There's a huge line of people waiting. We stop over to say hello. Mr. Johnson waves while Barry fixes plates for everyone.

"How y'all doing, familia Torres?"

"Doin' all right, Trey," my dad says. "Smells as amazing as always."

"Man, I tell you, thank goodness for these festivals. Folks *love* this food!"

"They sure do. How's the loan application coming along for your restaurant?"

"It's coming," Mr. Johnson says. "Slow, but what can we do? At least these festivals bring in some money."

"Yep," Papi says. "Well, you let me know if I can help in any way."

"You bet. Hey, come by the house on Sunday after church. We're having a small cookout. Just close friends and family."

Papi nods. "We'll be there."

It's the first invitation he's accepted since he's returned. Mr. Johnson cuts off a little piece of meat and hands it to me. I take a bite and it's like the world slows down so I can savor every bit of tangy, homemade sauce.

"So great," I say between bites.

Mami starts to sing as we walk down the street.

"What are you singing, Mami?"

"Just an old song from Cuba. Bet you'll never guess where it comes from?"

"From the Yoruba?"

"You got it," she says.

She sings another verse before she says, "I'm so happy here with my family." I take her hand so she knows I feel the same way too. "Mi amor, the Bay Area has so many great places to explore. I want us all to visit so you can see how cool it is!"

I try not to say anything as we walk. Papi and Abuela seem to be doing the same. I guess we're letting Mom have the excitement she deserves.

She's been talking nonstop about San Francisco even though she hasn't accepted the job offer. I overheard her telling my dad about her potential salary and benefits and the great schools. I'm still not sure how I feel about it, because it's all happening at once. Maybe life happens that way sometimes. One minute, it's like it's always been, and the next, you realize how different everything has become.

The bandstand on Main Street is decked out with mini train sets and there are booths everywhere selling locally made products. The school pep band warms up in the corner, with kids running all around, but I don't see Clarissa.

"The neighborhoods in the Bay Area are amazing," Mom says. "There's one right by a few huge tech companies that feels just like Merryville, only it has more coffee shops and a bookstore!"

We walk up to Jimmy's booth—they're selling shakes.

"Plus," Mami continues, "I *cannot wait* to shake up the tech boys' club and bring a new point of view to the table. ¿Verdad?"

"Can't argue with that," Papi says.

"Shakes all around!" Mom yells, like a boss.

I give her an *Are you sure?* look.

"Yes, I'm sure," she says. "We have lots to celebrate."

"Like what?"

"Being together, for one," Papi says.

Papi looks at Mami lovingly for a moment before he takes her hand and kisses it.

After the festival, we all huddle on the back porch and gaze out at the town. I look at the Shelby in the back lot and wonder when we'll finish it.

"So much has changed, huh?" I say, nestled between Mami and Papi on the porch swing while Abuela sits in her Adirondack chair, looking quietly toward town. The little lights on Main Street twinkle against the woods that lead to Park View. Mom rests her head on Papi's shoulder, and I lean on his other arm.

I take out a piece of Diana nougat fresa candy from my pocket and unwrap it. Mom lifts her head off Papi's shoulder. I remember that we already drank milkshakes, so I go to put it back in my pocket.

"You can have it, mi amor," she says. "Just this once."

I finish unwrapping it and put the whole thing in my mouth, in case she changes her mind. I rest my head on

Papi and everything is quiet except for the Diana nougat skipping in my mouth like a flat rock across a river. My head bobs up and down as Papi's tummy starts bouncing and then I hear Mom laugh. Abuela looks over and just shakes her head.

# CHAPTER TWENTY-FIVE

The next morning, after church, I tell Mom and Dad that I want to go to the library to thank Mrs. Liz for all her help.

"It's open on Sunday?"

"Yeah, it's closed on Thursdays but open the rest of the week."

"Didn't know that," Mom says.

Gus and his family find us when Mass is over. They're going to meet us at the barbecue at Barry's house later.

"See you there, Señorita Emilia," Gus says.

"Hasta luego, Señor Gustavo."

Mom and Dad decide to go for a walk, and Abuela stays behind to help out with the next service.

"See you at home, Chispita," Papi tells me.

"¿Chispita?" Mom asks.

"We've been working on the Shelby together," Papi explains, "and we came up with a new nickname."

"Little spark, huh? I like it."

Papi winks.

"Did you know," Mom says, "that your dad bought that car fourteen years ago?"

"Really?"

Papi nods.

"He said he would plan to work on it during every leave, and when he got out of service, he and I were going to drive it across the country."

"Why didn't you finish it back then, Papi?"

"Well," he says, "I ended up having something better to come home to."

"What?"

"You."

My dad can cast spells. Sometimes, like now, they make me feel like I'm floating. I don't think my feet are touching the ground.


At the library, Mrs. Liz tells me about the changes she wants to make. She wants to host language classes once a week, and she wants to make space for the community to organize and talk about policy. I tell her those are great ideas.

"Thanks for helping me with my project, Mrs. Liz."

"It's my pleasure, Emilia," Mrs. Liz replies. "You asked good questions. I just tried to point you in the right direction."

I take in a big breath of musty books. It might be one of my favorite smells now.

"My job is to make sure you have the information you need to make smart decisions as you move through the world," she says. "I take my job seriously. You can count on me for that."

Sometimes your community looks out for you. Like Mrs. Jenkins and her "check-ins" or Mrs. Liz showing me how to find information in the library. Sometimes people help in more subtle ways, like Mr. Richt and his social studies lessons. Sometimes it's more complicated, like Abuela and her rules.

I love Merryville *and* Park View. I love the way the trees surround us on all sides. The way the train tracks cut through town. The way people get too excited about fireworks or a school football game or a random festival.

There is good in this town, but you can't put together a vehicle with a messed-up bead line. You can't expect your car to drive normally with a damaged axle. You have to take it apart. You have to examine the pieces that are warped or corroded or missing. You have to grind out the corrosion. You must take a dead blow hammer and smash the warped parts into place.

At dinner that night, we all sit around the table. Abuela has prepared an enormous amount of food. Steak, yucca, white rice, plantains, black beans (gross), and flan de coco! Then she comes out with a platter of foot-long hot dogs and two bowls—one with chili and the other with shredded cheese.

"What's this?" Mom asks.

"I made something traditional," she says, pointing to the plate of Cuban food on the table. "And I made your favorite."

Abuela passes two hot dogs to Mom. She moves her hands away from the table so Abuela can set down the bowl of chili next to her. Mom leans forward a little to sniff the food. Her hair envelops the plate like a curtain, just missing the bowl.

"I *love* chili dogs," she says softly.

"You love chili *cheese* dogs," Abuela responds. She takes the ladle and drizzles chili over Mom's two hot dogs.

She tosses a pinch of freshly grated cheddar over it. We all watch as the cheese melts into the chili.

"Got any more of those?" Papi asks.

"You want a perro caliente también? Not this delicious Cuban food?"

"Yes," I chime in. "We definitely want those chili cheese dogs. With fries if you can, Abuela. Por favor."

Abuela gives me side eye before huffing and heading back into the kitchen. I overhear her say something about cultural heritage and what kind of person prefers chili to black beans. My dad and I shrug.

"We're also Georgians," Papi says.

"And we like our chili cheese dawgs," I say loud enough for Abuela to hear.

Papi cracks up when I say *dogs* like that. He says I'm from Georgia. I think he hopes I decide to go to the University of Georgia after high school, but I think I might be interested in Georgia Tech instead. Go Yellow Jackets.

We eat and chat about the week ahead. Mom doesn't pepper me with questions about homework. She just asks what the plan is for the week. I run down my list: homework, hanging out with Gus, working on the car. She seems happy with the way I've organized my time.

"When do you have to go back, Mom?"

Mom doesn't immediately respond. First she glances at my dad.

"I don't know if I want to take the job, baby," she says. "We're all finally back together, you know?"

I'm happy . . . but not completely.

"Well, we'll talk about it," Papi says. "Nothing is set yet."

Abuela comes in with two more plates of hot dogs and an even bigger bowl of chili. She struggles to bring everything to the table and ends up dropping the bowl. It crashes on the floor and shatters into pieces. Bits of chili splatter everywhere.

"Aye, Dios mío," Abuela says.

My dad is the first up. He heads to the kitchen and comes back with a roll of paper towels. He hands them to me and I get right to the floor and start scooping up the bits of chili.

"Careful with the glass," Mom says. She carefully picks up shards that have scattered everywhere.

"Déjame buscar el Mistolín," Abuela says, but before she enters the kitchen, Papi is two steps ahead of her. He returns with a mop and bucket.

"Wait until Emilia finishes, Antonio," Abuela says.

"Mami, siéntese." My dad motions for Abuela to sit down. "We got this."

Mom, Dad, and I work together to clean up the mess while Abuela watches. She points to broken pieces we miss or smudges we need to go over again. Dad pours so much Mistolín, it nearly sends us all out of the dining room from the potent lavender-lime.

We finish up and sit down to enjoy the meal. Papi returns from the kitchen with another bowl of chili. He serves Abuela and me and then pours some for himself. After Abuela says a prayer as thanks, we dig in.

It doesn't take us long to devour the chili dogs. Before we take our last bites, I decide to tell Mami what's on my mind.

"Mom?" I ask.

"¿Sí, mi amor?"

"I don't want to move to San Francisco. I want to stay here. In Merryville. This is my home."

I take a slow breath. I'm nervous about what she's going to say, but I want her to hear the truth.

"That's why I don't want to take the job, boo. You're thriving here. Why would I take that away? I mean we have everything—"

"But," I interrupt, preparing the second part of what I have to say, "you should take the job. We'll find time to visit you when you have to be away for long. And I know you'll come home as much as you can. We'll figure it out, Mami."

Mom doesn't respond right away. She lets everything sink in for a minute.

"Baby, I'm not going to just—"

"She's right, Susanna," Abuela jumps in. "It's a great opportunity. And we'll always be here for you."

Abuela gets up and moves behind my seat to squeeze my shoulder.

"Our families didn't sacrifice for us to hide our talents," Abuela says.

"It's your turn, Sue," Dad says. He knows she wants to be there. He knows that somehow we'll figure it out—like all the times he's left. That's what we do. We take all the pieces and we put them together. They morph into different shapes over time, but somehow, they'll all fit.

# CHAPTER TWENTY-SIX

Dad knocks on my door at around six on a Monday morning a few weeks later.

"Come in," I say, barely able to talk.

"You told me you wanted me to wake you up early."

He flips on my lamp and I turn to avoid the light. He walks in and sits on the edge of my bed.

"Good morning, Chispita."

"Hey, Papi," I say, still groggy.

Dad heads to my bathroom and returns to set a few things on my dresser. I peek and see that he's laid out my brush, a few bows, some hair ties, and some hair spray.

"You told me you wanted that one, right?"

"Yeah," I say. I move my covers off, throw my legs over the bed, and rub my eyes. Dad opens the curtains to let the early morning light wash in.

"All set for you, Chispita."

"Thanks, Papi."

"Anything else?"

"No, I'm good."

I give my dad a big hug.

"I'll make some café con leche," he says.

"Yummy."

I start my new morning routine. After I'm dressed, I move over to my dresser and take my hair products to the full-length mirror Papi set up in my room. I fluff my hair for maximum volume and add a little hair spray. When I'm done, I spritz on some body splash and bring my things back to my bathroom.

Papi returns with the pot of café and a cup for himself. Together we watch the trees and birds outside my window. It's a perfect moment, until Abuela pops in with a flatiron.

"¿Ya te levantastes?"

"Sí," I tell her.

"And she already did her hair, Mami," Dad says.

Abuela gives us both a look.

"Pero ¿cómo vas a ir al colegio así?"

"I told you, Aurelia. It's her choice." Mom appears over Abuela's shoulder.

I scrunch my hair a few more times so the curls settle around my shoulders. I admire myself in the mirror.

"Impressive," Papi says. "I love it."

I turn to Abuela and shrug.

"I like lions, Abuela," I tell her. "What can I say?"


Later that afternoon, Papi asks if I can join him in the living room. It's been a rough day, because Mom just left for the West Coast to start training for her new job. It's just me and Dad at the house because Abuela is at the auto shop.

Papi has his back to me as he fiddles with the TV. I'm not sure what's going on, but if we're about to watch a movie, I hope it's *Labyrinth*.

He seems to have queued up what he wanted because he joins me on the sofa. Papi is quiet, barely moving except when he rubs his hands together on his lap. I can't quite read his face. He's acting really weird.

I'm about to ask him what's up when the video starts to play.

# DAD'S VIDEO
## #1

Dad leans against his workbench. He's wearing his Marine-issued utility uniform and boots. His cover is resting on the workbench behind him, and he messes around with a wrench. He seems nervous as he stares into the camera. His name is on a strip of fabric stitched to the right side of his blouse. He shaved his beard and cut his hair short like it used to be. In the dark of the garage, he could still be on tour somewhere thousands of miles away.

"Um, well, here it goes," he says. "Hang on—let me make sure this thing is recording."

He walks over to the camera and out of view. The workbench comes in and out of focus as he adjusts the lens. The camera rustles a few more times before Dad comes back around. The late spring wind brushes against the beech trees just outside the garage. The shop is closed, but there's something like a low-budget spotlight on my dad.

"Okay, take two," he says.

He inhales and closes his eyes. The camera catches every movement as he exhales. Finally he opens his mouth to state his rank.

"Staff Sergeant Antonio Torres," he says. He goes on to list his company and the tours he did during his twelve years in the Marine Corps.

"Actually, I don't know why I'm stating all of this. You know who I am, and you know more or less how many times I've been away from you and Mom and Abuela. I know you sent those videos, and I want to tell you right now that I saw every single one of them."

Papi pauses to think before continuing.

"The thing is, I severed myself from my family so I could fight. Sometimes I didn't want to hear from back home. When you're out there and you're seeing action, getting fired on from all directions, you just assume that that moment could be your last. You feel a kind of numbness inside."

My chest starts to feel heavy. I watch my dad struggling to continue.

"Emilia, it was hard for me to think about home while I was out there. I felt like one person with my unit and

313

another totally different one back home. I haven't figured out how to balance everything, but I'm going to try harder. I promise."

Papi clenches his jaw like I do when I'm stressed or angry.

"I should have responded to you. I should have sent you a video every dang chance I got because what good is fighting to protect the ones you love if you can't show your love?"

Papi's eyes are red and I can tell he's fighting back tears. I feel my own eyes welling up. He holds his gaze at the camera and nods before walking out of frame. The video keeps rolling and I see the welder off to the side and the dead blow hammer and clamps organized neatly on the workbench.

"I'm having a hard time right now," he offers, coming back into frame and looking at the camera. "You know how sometimes you have trouble focusing on one thought when there are lots of thoughts in your head? Like when you're trying to do homework or take notes?"

I nod at my dad on the TV.

"Well, the same thing is happening with my feelings." His head drops and his shoulders sag. "I'm feeling a lot of things right now, and I'm having trouble controlling which feelings get out and which ones don't. Does that make sense?"

He pauses to catch his breath, letting the tears fall down his cheeks.

"But I know it's not fair to you and Abuela and Mami. So I want you to know that I *am* going to get help. I *do* care about how this is affecting you. Okay?"

I move my hand across the sofa and give Dad's hand a gentle squeeze. He turns his palm upward and takes my hand in his. We don't say anything or even look at each other. We don't have to.

# AUTHOR'S NOTE

This book is a work of fiction. Many aspects of the novel, however, are drawn from research on subjects ranging from finding reliable news resources to immigration law to neurodiversity to our nation's veterans and active duty military. These are all important topics that affect the lives of children and families from varying socioeconomic, racial, and cultural backgrounds. Knowledge is power, and I hope the list of resources below will be a useful tool to, as Mr. Richt says, "dig deeper" into the important themes explored in *Each Tiny Spark*.

## CRITICAL READING

Society of Professional Journalists Code of Ethics
www.spj.org

There is a great deal of information (and in many cases, misinformation) available today. SPJ's Code of Ethics is one tool to help determine the credibility of an article or news organization. The code includes the following four principles: "seek truth and report it," "minimize harm," "act independently," "be accountable and transparent."

## WIRE SERVICES LIKE
## ASSOCIATED PRESS AND REUTERS

A wire service is an organization that supplies news to newspapers, radio, and television stations electronically. Most news content comes from wire services, and I incorporated them into the scenes where Emilia reads archived news stories for her history project.

Also, I would encourage readers to subscribe to their local newspapers (as Emilia does through her library). This will help these news organizations employ journalists who attend city hall and school board meetings, and who hold elected officials accountable.

# NATIONAL IMMIGRANTS' RIGHTS ORGANIZATIONS

American Civil Liberties Union (ACLU)

www.aclu.org

The ACLU has existed for almost 100 years. This nonprofit and nonpartisan organization works to defend the individual rights and liberties guaranteed to everyone in this country by the Constitution and laws of the United States. There is an ACLU chapter in every state, and I encourage readers to look up their own state chapters to learn more about what's happening in their communities. It certainly helps Emilia!

Anti-Defamation League

www.adl.org

The Anti-Defamation League was first created in the early 1900s to combat anti-Semitism (discrimination and prejudice against Jews). The league's current mission is to "secure justice and fair treatment to all."

National Immigration Law Center

www.nilc.org

It is the mission of the National Immigration Law Center to fight against policies that ignore the fundamental rights of immigrants. They aim to do this through research, policy analysis, litigation, and community resources.

## RESOURCES FOR NEURODIVERSITY

Child Mind Institute
www.childmind.org

The Child Mind Institute is an independent nonprofit organization that helps children and families struggling with mental health and learning disorders. According to their research, "of the 74.5 million children living in the United States, an estimated 17.1 million have or have had a mental disorder." By conducting research on brain development and sharing resources with parents and educators, the Child Mind Institute is doing great work in the field.

Emilia, like my own daughter, has Attention Deficit Hyperactivity Disorder. Resources from the Child Mind Institute helped me capture the way a child with ADHD becomes intensely focused on something that interests them. This is why Emilia sometimes has trouble with Language Arts homework, for example, which does not interest her as much as Mr. Richt's class.

Children and Adults with Attention-Deficit/Hyperactivity Disorder (CHADD)
www.chadd.org

CHADD is a national nonprofit that provides education, advocacy, and support for individuals with ADHD. The organization also publishes a number of printed materials to inform on current ADHD research.

## VETERANS SUPPORT ORGANIZATIONS

Bob Woodruff Foundation
https://bobwoodrufffoundation.org/

Bob Woodruff was a journalist who was critically injured while reporting in 2006. During his recovery, he and his wife were introduced to many families of service members dealing with post-traumatic stress and traumatic brain injuries. The Woodruff family created this foundation to help military service members and veterans struggling with these issues and many more.

Semper Fi Fund
www.semperfifund.org

This highly rated charity is dedicated to providing critical support and resources to members of the U.S. Armed Forces and their families in need.

United Service Organizations (USO)
www.uso.org

The USO supports active military and veterans with many programs and services. They are known for the shows they put on to entertain troops, but they also help soldiers stay connected to their families and assist with the transition back into their communities after service. Take a look at the "Stories" section of their website for real-life accounts and profiles about individuals and families of members serving in our Armed Forces.

Okay, Reader: go, find your spark.

All my best,
Pablo

# ACKNOWLEDGMENTS

This book needs a whole other chapter to cover the gratitude I have to the people and organizations that helped me realize my vision for this story.

To my publisher, Namrata Tripathi, and the incredibly talented team at Kokila. You challenge, you question, you support, you set a high standard, and for this I am a better writer and ever grateful to be part of such an important imprint. Also, a BIG shout-out to the Penguin Young Readers team, including the School & Library department; my publicist, Kaitlin Kneafsey; and so many others. You are all rock stars and I am so grateful to you for putting my books out into the world. ¡Mil gracias!

My many thanks to my editor, Joanna Cárdenas. THREE BOOKS together and every single one has been an incredible journey. You understand my work and push hard to help me get the story where it needs to be. Eres un tesoro.

To my agent, Jess Regel, and the team at Foundry Literary + Media, thank you for your support. Jess, you are more than an agent. You're an advocate, a supporter, a dear, dear friend.

I did a great deal of research for this book and there are a few individuals I'd like to give a shout-out to.

Vanessa Walker-Wilfong, mi hermana, who has worked in the Georgia Public School system since 2005 and who spent countless hours with me talking about Georgia Education standards, rules, regulations, and more. There are not enough words—or pastelitos—I can offer to express my love and gratitude. Te quiero.

My sincerest thanks to the following people for their consultation on the military aspects of the novel: USMC Lieutenant Colonel Benjamin Busch, a friend and darn good actor, author, and all-around great human; the incredible

Brian Turner, writer and US Army combat veteran; and Ray Ramos, Army Vietnam veteran. In addition, I want to thank the Wounded Warrior Project, an organization that is there for veterans as they take their first steps into civilian life. I truly appreciate the work you do for our veterans.

A special thanks to Dr. Cristina Rhodes, who provided a wealth of academic papers and incredible resources to pore through about neurodiversity and Afro-Caribbean studies to help me dig even deeper. ¡Gracias!

A huge thank you to sculptor, cartoonist, installation artist, and teacher, Shing Yin Khor, who shared essential feedback on the welding scenes between Emilia and her father. My work is better for her careful observations and suggestions. I'd also like to thank the American Welding Society, which made available countless lessons on welding and handbooks that I'm still trying to decipher.

Señor Pedro Cárdenas, sir, I owe you a tremendous thanks. You gave sooo many great suggestions and details about the auto body shop business. ¡Gracias! Oh, and I hear you also make a mean paella so, I may be asking for some tips on that as well, if that's okay with you. :)

Big shout-out to Daniel José Older for helping me understand the nuance of Santeria language as well as my sister-in-law, Kiany Cartaya, and brother-in-law, Ramon Alexis Monje, for your insight into the character of Emilia's mother and her Santera roots. Much respect and love to you all.

To my mother, who is strong, and loving, and unwavering in her commitment to her family. Mami: you left once to pursue an opportunity and I'm so proud that I get to experience your shine. Te quiero.

Thank you, Papi, for your lessons, talks, and quiet determination in the face of great difficulty. To my brothers, Danny and Guillo, and my extended family and friends: as always, thank you for your support and love. Los quiero mucho. Y gracias a Abuelo y Abuela for always protecting us.

To my daughter and son, who are the models for Emilia and Gus: you are kind and smart and so much better than

I ever was at your age. I am in awe of you. And thank you to my little Paloma, who has only just arrived and is already making an impact for good. And, as always, to the woman who gives meaning to everything I do: Rebecca, eres todo.

# A Discussion Guide to
# PABLO CARTAYA

THE EPIC FAIL OF
ARTURO ZAMORA

MARCUS VEGA
DOESN'T SPEAK SPANISH

EACH TINY SPARK

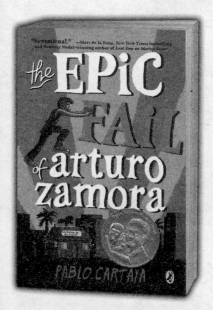

# DISCUSSION QUESTIONS

1. This novel begins with Arturo's "Note to Self." What is the effect of the book beginning here?

2. Why is food so important to Arturo and his family?

3. Look at Chapter 4, "Ice Scream: a Dialogue." This chapter is very different from the rest of the novel. Why did the author choose to make this almost like a play with dialogue and stage directions?

4. Who was José Martí? Why is he so important for this book?

5. Carmen's protest sign reads "FAMILY IS COMMUNITY—COMMUNITY IS FAMILY." What does this mean?

6. After Arturo is upset because he feels like he failed, he takes a moment to directly address the reader of his book. "Dear reader, I told you not to be fooled by high expectations." Why do you think he talks directly to the reader? Did you feel like he was talking to you? Explain.

7. What are Arturo's epic fails? How do they impact him, and those around him, throughout the story?

8. Is Wilfrido Pipo evil? Why or why not?

9. Why does Arturo decide to use a poem to address the neighborhood?

# EXTENSION ACTIVITIES

Arturo, Carmen, and Arturo's family protest Pipo's proposed plan. While their involvement is on a large scale, think of something that's happening in your own community and create a protest sign to advocate for yourself, your class, your school, or whoever! On the back of the sign, explain the history of the situation and propose an idea for how to fix it. (CCSS.ELA-LITERACY.WHST.6-8.1, CCSS.ELA LITERACY.WHST.6-8.2)

Arturo's abuelo leaves him letters. Write a letter to your own future relatives—tell about a time when you made a difference in the world and give your future relative wisdom about how they could be a changemaker. (CCSS.ELA-LITERACY.W.6.3)

# One boy's search for his father leads him to Puerto Rico, in this moving middle-grade novel.

Marcus Vega is six feet tall, 180 pounds, and the owner of a premature mustache. When you look like this and you're only in the eighth grade, you're both a threat and a target.

After a fight at school leaves Marcus facing suspension, Marcus's mom decides it's time for a change of environment. She takes Marcus and his younger brother to Puerto Rico to spend a week with relatives they don't remember or have never met. But Marcus can't focus knowing that his father—who walked out of their lives ten years ago—is somewhere on the island.

Marcus's journey takes him all over Puerto Rico. He doesn't know if he'll ever find his father, but what he ultimately discovers changes his life. And he even learns a bit of Spanish along the way.

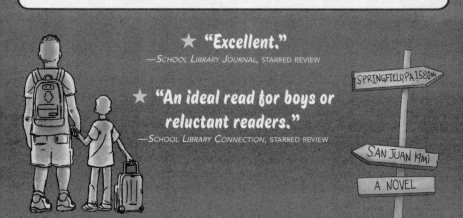

# DISCUSSION QUESTIONS

1. When we are introduced to Marcus, he's described as "the Mastodon of Montgomery Middle, the Springfield Skyscraper, the Moving Mountain, the Terrible Tower," but his actions and care for his brother contradict these images of him as a big monster. How would you describe Marcus instead?

2. Why does Principal Jenkins suggest Charlie attend another school?

3. Marcus's businesses help enforce school rules. Is it wrong that he's making money by doing this? Explain.

4. Do you think Danny's petition to keep Marcus in school was useful? Why did Danny start this petition?

5. Why does Marcus's mother eventually decide that the family should go to Puerto Rico?

6. The book is called *Marcus Vega Doesn't Speak Spanish*, and throughout the novel Marcus himself admits that he doesn't know the language. Is this true? Do you think Marcus doesn't know Spanish? Explain.

7. How do you feel about the fact that much of the Spanish dialogue isn't translated? Why might the author have chosen to not include an English translation or glossary?

8. Marcus gets angry a few times during this book—he punches Stephen, and later he also punches Sergio's truck. What could he do to better channel his emotions?

9. What does Charlie mean when he tells his father, "You broke the rules!" after he tries to explain his absence to Marcus?

10. Marcus observes that Puerto Rico changed his mom: "This post–Puerto Rico Mom is fierce. Who knew beautiful weather, old architecture, a gorgeous countryside, and exotic fruits and vegetables could do that to a person?" Do you think Puerto Rico changed Marcus and Charlie, too? If so, how?

## EXTENSION ACTIVITIES

In the Author's Note at the end of the book, Pablo Cartaya explains that this book represents a Puerto Rico before it was devastated by hurricanes in 2017. Knowing that Puerto Rico's landscape was so changed by these events, do some research on Puerto Rico before and after the hurricanes and write a compare and contrast report explaining the significant changes to the island after these events. (CCSS.ELA-LITERACY.RST.6-8.1, CCSS.ELA-LITERACY.W.6.7, CCSS.ELA-LITERACY.RI.5.6)

Keeping in mind the travel guides Charlie gets in the airport for Puerto Rico, create your own travel guide for the island. Your guide should incorporate images, text, and other elements to encourage travelers to visit Puerto Rico. (CCSS.ELA-LITERACY.WHST.6-8.4, CCSS.ELA-LITERACY.WHST.6-8.6)

# A sparkling middle grade novel about a daughter and father finding their way back to each other in the face of their changing family and community.

Emilia Torres has a wandering mind. It's hard for her to follow along at school, and sometimes she forgets to do what her mom or abuela asks. But she remembers what matters: a time when her family was whole and home made sense. When Dad returns from deployment, Emilia expects that her life will get back to normal. Instead, it unravels.

Dad shuts himself in the back stall of their family's auto shop to work on an old car. Emilia peeks in on him daily, mesmerized by his welder. One day, Dad calls Emilia over. Then he teaches her how to weld. And over time, flickers of her old dad reappear.

But as Emilia finds a way to repair the relationship with her father at home, her community ruptures, with some of her classmates, like her best friend, Gus, at the center of the conflict.

# DISCUSSION QUESTIONS

1.  Why does Emilia record videos to send to her father when he is deployed?

2.  Emilia and her family drink café con leche, Cuban coffee. Her mother says that the smell of it is "'the sweet aroma of our island [Cuba] and our ancestors.'" What does that mean?

3.  Why does Emilia choose to begin her tour at the Latino food store?

4.  When Emilia discovers that the Olympic stadium was built by immigrants who then risked deportation, she wonders about the fate of her family members who are immigrants. She thinks: "Who makes the rules about who gets to stay somewhere and who has to leave?" This is a big question. Should someone have the power to dictate where others live? If they stay or go?

5.  Why do you think many students in Emilia's class don't know about the history of Park View and Merryville?

6.  Why does Gus forgive Emilia for standing him up at Clarissa's party?

7.  Why does Mr. Richt cancel the travel brochure project?

8.  Eventually, Emilia Rosa insists that Clarissa call her by her real name, instead of "Emi Rose." Why is it so important that Emilia Rosa be called by her real, full name?

9.  Describe Emilia's relationships with her family (mother, father, and grandmother). Why would she be okay with her mother taking the job in San Fransisco when her family is so rarely all together?

10. Emilia's father makes her a video at the end of the book. How does Emilia react to this video?

# EXTENSION ACTIVITIES

Emilia and Gus's video makes a big impact on their school, and Mr. Richt even hopes to share it with the community. In keeping with this moment in the text, make a video, like Emilia and Gus, about something going on at your school. The videos should include interviews and other footage relevant to the topic. (CCSS.ELA-LITERACY.RH.6-8.7)

So many of Pablo Cartaya's books seek to understand familial connections, but they also highlight the families that we make for ourselves that often transcend biological relations. Keeping this in mind, create family trees (both biological and chosen), doing research on your family archives to construct relations and see connections. These projects should be creative and should be accompanied by a brief, reflective writing where you explain your creative processes. (CCSS.ELA-LITERACY.WHST.6-8.10, CCSS.ELA-LITERACY.W.5.5, CCSS.ELA-LITERACY.W.5.7)

# About
# PABLO CARTAYA

Pablo Cartaya is an award-winning author, speaker, actor, and educator. In 2018, he received a Pura Belpré Author Honor for his middle grade novel *The Epic Fail of Arturo Zamora*. His second novel, *Marcus Vega Doesn't Speak Spanish*, is available now. His third novel, *Each Tiny Spark*, published in 2019 and is the recipient of the Schneider Family Book Award Honor for Middle Grade. Learn more about Pablo at pablocartaya.com and follow him on Twitter @phcartaya.

*PenguinClassroom.com*

 PenguinClassroom     @PenguinClass     PenguinClassroom

This guide was written by Cristina Rhodes. Cristina is an incoming assistant professor of ethnic literature. Her research explores Latinx youth identities and activism in children's literature.